Stink Bomb Mom

Stink Bomb Mom

MARTHA FREEMAN

Delacorte Press

Published by
Delacorte Press
Bantam Doubleday Dell Publishing Group, Inc.
1540 Broadway
New York, New York 10036

Library of Congress Cataloging-in-Publication Data
Freeman, Martha.
    Stink bomb mom / Martha Freeman.
      p.   cm.
    Summary: Constantly embarrassed by her eccentric mother,
Rory finds solace with her many pets and wonders what it would be
like to live with the departed father she hardly knows.
    ISBN 0-385-32219-4 (alk. paper)
    [1. Mothers and daughters—Fiction.   2. Single-parent family—
Fiction.   3. Pets—Fiction.]   I. Title.
PZ7.F87496St 1996   95-53355
[Fic]—dc20   CIP
                                                    AC

The text of this book is set in 14-point Berling Roman.
Manufactured in the United States of America
November 1996
10 9 8 7 6 5 4 3 2 1
BVG

For Russell

one

"I hate Pookie Tunnbaum." *Splat.*

"Hate 'er, hate 'er, hate 'er." *Splat*—another white gob of peppermint foam hits the washbasin.

Splat.

I rinse my mouth and shoot water at my reflection in the mirror. Then I narrow my eyes and pull my lips back into a snarl.

I look pretty fierce, as fierce as Agnes does when she sees a cat. Too bad my teeth aren't as sharp as a dog's. If Pookie could see me now, she'd run away and never come back. And good riddance.

Pookie Tunnbaum is my best friend.

Was my best friend. Until today, when she called my mom Dippy Doria in front of practically the whole sixth grade. It was at lunch. I had just opened my lunchbox, and inside it, along with the lunch I'd packed myself, was this little plastic marble full of liquid—like the oily things you throw in bathwater to smell it all up. Well, I knew what it was right away, and I tried to hide it with the raisins, but Pookie saw it.

"Golly molly, Rory!" she said to me—so loud I bet Mr. Goode in the principal's office could hear. "Not in your lunch! What does ol' Dippy Doria expect you to do? Cram it up your nose?"

Everybody at the whole table—including Sam, the new boy with the freckles—laughed. I would've dropped dead from embarrassment if I hadn't been so mad. So I just picked up my lunch, rose from the bench, and went off to eat by myself.

I thought Pookie would call after school to say she was sorry, but she didn't. And that's fine by me.

I hate her.

I'm the only one allowed to call my mom Dippy Doria. And I would never say it in front of all those people.

2

After I brush my teeth, I give Hedda and Hopper their nightly crickets; then I pull Agnes's leash off its hook in my closet. I'm about to call her when there's an *EEEEEE-eeeeep EEEEEE-eeeeep* from one of the cages.

"What'samatter, Costello? Huh?" I bend down to check. "Did Abby bite you again?" Abby looks harmless enough, but last week she dug those sharp little teeth right into Costello's defenseless little ear, and he EEEEE-eeeeped like crazy. Dr. Eshman—she's my vet—told me I oughta split them up, but I decided to give them one more chance. They've been together a long time.

I undo the latch, open the door, reach in, and catch Costello. He is not real sure about being grabbed, but I get a firm grip. He wiggles his pink feet like he's trying to swim in the air. I can see that both ears are fine and the rest of him too. I touch my nose to his fur so he knows he's not in trouble or anything, then lock him back in.

"Remember, Abby," I say sternly to his sweetie. "I'm watching you."

Now where's Agnes? She knows I always take her for a walk right before I go to bed.

3

My animals count on me, so I have to stick to my schedule.

Click-click-click-click-click-click. Here she comes—that's the sound of her toenails on the floor. She must've been napping in her spot behind the big blue chair in the living room.

I hook the leash on Agnes's collar. Before we go, I peek in the rat cage to see whether Robin has popped her pups yet. She hasn't.

"Going out with Agnes, Doria!" I call as my dog and I pass her bedroom. The door is closed, but I can still smell it—cinnamon tonight. It was some kind of tropical flower this morning.

"All right, darling!" Doria answers. "May the moon goddess illuminate your path!"

Moon goddess. *Honestly.*

On the front steps, the moon goddess, if there is such a person, provides about a half-moon's worth of light to help the street-lamps. It's cold, and even with my parka on over my pajamas I shiver. But walking will warm me up.

"Right or left, ol' girl?" I ask at the foot of our walk.

Agnes flaps her batwing ears and tugs left. She's a broad, brown mutt, the same age as me—old for a dog. But she barks like a pup when Mr. Cinnamon comes to the door with another Cinnamon Seminars package for Mom. She doesn't like Cinnamon Seminars either.

"Shoulda known," I say as we start down the sidewalk. "The zoo again."

The only trouble with walking to the zoo is we go right by Pookie's house on the way back. The trouble with that is, first, I hate Pookie so much I don't even want to see her bedroom window. Second, one night last week when we walked by her house I heard her parents shouting bloody murder at each other. I felt like I was snooping. And I felt sad.

Lots of houses have dogs, and Agnes's toenails click-clicking down the sidewalk set them off one by one. We're followed by a chorus of barking and people shouting, "Shut up and lie down!" People shouldn't talk to their dogs like that. I never talk to Agnes like that.

Nearer the zoo, the houses are not so nice

and the front yards are messy. Agnes likes these best. She makes me stop at practically every one so she can sniff around and see if any of her friends has left her a message. Pookie says dogs are gross, but I say dogs are dogs.

We cross Dingo Boulevard and walk by a car part store, a deli, a Chinese restaurant, and a little grocery store. It was around here about a month ago that Agnes found half a Big Mac in a vacant lot. Now we stop and look for the other half whenever we go by.

My street, Puma Street, runs into Zoo Drive. We have to cross it to get to the zoo. As usual, Agnes yanks so hard on the leash that I give in, and we walk along the zoo fence for a block. Through the shrubs on the other side of the fence are the big cats— lions, tigers, cougars. Tonight Agnes sniffs at that chain-link like a vacuum cleaner and whines so loud she practically howls.

"Come on, ol' girl." I pull her away so we can cross back in the other direction. "Those kitties are king-size. It'd be bad news if you ever met one."

Sometimes we meet some grown-up who

says, "Isn't it awfully late for you to be out by yourself, honey?" And I say, "I'm not by myself. I'm with my dog."

One time somebody asked about my pajamas. *Honestly.* How rude. It isn't as though flannel pajamas are *indecent* or something. But I guess most parents don't let their kids walk the dog in their pajamas after dark. The thing about Doria is, she hasn't a clue what most parents do.

We're almost to Pookie's house. She lives on Bengal, right around the corner from my house. I can see the light on in her room, in front on the second floor. I think about picking up a rock and heaving it right through the window. *Pow!*

We're almost past her house when I think I hear the creak of a window opening. Agnes growls.

"Rory! Rory Mudd!" Pookie's voice is sort of a shouted whisper. "Wait! I'll be right down." Pookie's parents would never in a zillion years let her walk a dog at night, not that they'd ever let her have a dog to walk.

Agnes snarls again when the front door

opens. She must've picked up on how mad I am at Pookie. Dogs are sensitive that way. "Quiet, Agnes! Shusssshhhh. Her parents'll hear you."

Agnes quiets down, but there's still that rumble in the pit of her throat. Pookie's running right at me, her white nightgown flying. I hope she slows down. I bend down to put my arm around Agnes just as Pookie hits the sidewalk and steps hard on Agnes's front paw.

"Rory, I— Yo-o-o-o-ow! Call 'er off! Call 'er off! Rory-y-y-y-y-y!"

"You stepped right on her!"

Oh man, what a mess we're in now! Agnes bit Pookie right on the leg. I'm trying to separate them and see how bad the damage is to Pookie.

"She didn't mean it, Pookie," I say. Pookie is crying. "But you stepped on her foot! You're gonna be okay. Really."

The funny thing is, Pookie's saying practically the same thing: "I'm sorry, Rory. It was my fault. I never should've said that at lunch."

Of course lights are blinking on in the

Tunnbaum house. Pookie screamed loud as a fire siren. You'd've thought Agnes at least killed her.

"Does it hurt bad? I don't see any blood."

"I'm not crying about that. I'm crying about how much trouble I'm gonna get in."

And right on schedule, here comes Mr. Tunnbaum. He's the mayor, which is why, I guess, he's the only dad I ever met who makes me call him Mr.

"What's the meaning of this? Priscilla? Aurora?" Priscilla is Pookie's real name. Aurora's mine. Only grown-ups ever use them. And usually only if they're mad.

Agnes is growling again. I get a good grip on her. "Quiet, ol' girl," I say, and she shuts right up. She must feel bad about biting Pookie too.

Pookie's still in tears when her dad gets to us, and his face softens up a little. "What happened, honey?"

"Agnes bit her," I say.

Pookie sniffles. "It's okay, Daddy. . . ."

"Bit you! Let me see! Are you bleeding? That dog is a menace! I've always said so!"

Actually, I don't think Mr. Tunnbaum

9

ever cared enough to say anything about Agnes. But right now he's looking at her like she's got rabies. Agnes doesn't look too happy with Mr. Tunnbaum either, but at least *she's* stopped growling.

"It was an accident," I say. "Agnes never bit anybody before. She thought she was protecting me. And Pookie stepped right on her. She's probably hurt more than Pookie is."

This is the wrong thing to say. Mr. Tunnbaum kicks Agnes—*kicks my dog*—right in the ribs. She yowls, then snarls and tries to get back at his ankle. He is prancing backward as he says, "Get that mongrel out of here or I'll see to it she is hurt more than Priscilla is."

He turns to Pookie and starts in on her as he herds her back toward the house. "And what were you doing outside at this time of night anyway, young lady . . . ?"

Mrs. Tunnbaum appears at the front door. She's yelling something in that high-pitched voice of hers, and it sounds about like another dog whining. Nobody's paying any attention to me, so I make my escape.

10

I hope Agnes is okay. I feel sorry for Pookie. She can be my best friend. All I wanted was for her to say she was sorry, and she did.

two

Seven o'clock. Agnes leans her front paws up against the side of the bed and pokes my face with her cold wet nose.

She wants to go out in the backyard. Agnes is like me. She sticks to her schedule.

I roll out of bed and walk her to the back door. She's not limping or anything. I guess Mr. Tunnbaum's kick didn't hurt her much. When I prodded her ribs last night, she barely complained.

It's Saturday, the day I wash Agnes and change the water in the fishbowl. Like every morning, I've also got to change the cedar shavings and newspaper in the cages and the litter in the cat boxes, and feed and water everybody.

Doria told me yesterday she's hosting her first Cinnamon Seminar this afternoon. I think she's nervous. If I were going to try to sell little tiny stink bombs to a bunch of total strangers, I'd be nervous too. Anyway, my plan is to get the chores done pronto and get out of here. Maybe I can do something with Pookie.

Of course I'm dying to know how much trouble she's in and if Agnes really hurt her knee. But I can't call till later. Pookie always sleeps in on weekends.

I go out to the garage to get the old newspapers and the bag of shavings. Then I load it all in a cardboard box. I keep steel wool, sponges, bleach, and a bucket under the sink in my bathroom.

Back in my room, I look at my animals. Most of them are busy—either cracking sunflower seeds, jogging in their whirly-wheels, or climbing the bars of the cages like they're jungle gyms.

"Okay," I say, "who wants to be first?"

It's tough to tell anything from a guinea

pig's expression. Mostly they look pinched. But I think I see the tiniest hint of enthusiasm from Laurel and Hardy, so I start with them.

First I pull out the drawer under their cage. Then I crumple the dirty newspaper and shavings in a wad and put it in the cardboard box. Then I scrub anything that needs to be scrubbed, put in sheets of clean newspaper, and sprinkle on clean cedar shavings. While I'm on guinea pigs, I do the rest of the guinea pigs too—Laurel and Hardy's two children and four grandchildren, who live in the cages next door.

Actually it's not that bad a job as long as you do it every day. I like the smell of newspaper and cedar. The animals like it too.

When they're all clean, I pick up Laurel— she's the one with black spots—and touch her nose to mine. She burbles at me. Must be hungry.

"I'll come back with clean water and your pellets. Maybe I can even find you a piece of parsley, if Doria went to the store," I tell her. That parsley sounds good. I can tell because Laurel wrinkles her nose at me.

Laurel was one of the first animals I bought. That was almost two years ago, right when Doria went to work for the library cataloging old movies. We used to watch them together, which is where I got a lot of the animals' names.

Three down. Only twelve cages, the terrariums, two litter boxes, the bathtub, and the fishbowl to go.

I guess I have a lot of animals. The bookshelves in my room are lined with cages, so I had to put most of the books in the garage. My alarm clock sits on top of the mouse cage on the table by my bed. Margaret Hamilton's terrarium takes up most of my desk, so I do my homework on the floor. And with Hedda and Hopper in the bathtub, I usually use Doria's shower.

The thing about animals is, if you have a boy and a girl, you're gonna have a whole lot more before long. Take Larry and Vivien, my gerbils. They're two years old, and they can pop a litter every month. Now, if every pair of baby gerbils pops out more baby gerbils . . . well, it's a lot of gerbils. For a while there, Doria was afraid we'd have to

15

buy a new house, especially because I absolutely refuse to give any of my animals away. I don't trust anybody but me to take good care of them.

Anyway, after the first couple of litters I discovered the secret of gerbil population control: separate cages for boys and girls. This also works for the other rodents.

Abby and Costello still share because they're almost two years old, over the hill for smooching if you're a mouse. My other original pairs—Larry and Vivien, Laurel and Hardy, and Edward G. and Robin—still share too, but they have separate bedrooms. Wire mesh separates the halves of the cage. Of course every once in a while there's a slip-up, which is how come I have, at last count, sixteen gerbils, eleven mice, eight guinea pigs, twelve hamsters, and five rats. It's also how come Robin the rat is expecting again.

Doria, who doesn't really care much about animals, can't tell one from another and just calls them all gerbils—even the snakes. She was the one who started calling my room Gerbil City.

"Next?" I ask. Margaret Hamilton winks one green eyelid and sticks out her red tongue, so I go to her terrarium.

I turn off her heat lamp—"just for a minute, Margaret"—and drape her over my shoulder so I can replace her litter. "Nice iguana," I say. "I saved a wormy apple for you. Yummy!"

Margaret is a vegetarian, like Doria, and she's a lot of work. She mainly eats Iguana Chow, but I cut up a few pieces of fruit for her every day too. Kiwi fruit is her favorite. Iguanas can grow up to six feet long, but she's still young, only a couple of feet, and two thirds of her is tail.

While I work, Margaret rests quietly on my shoulder, sticking her tongue out now and then. When it's all clean I put her back in her terrarium and turn the heat lamp back on. She crawls up on her branch and winks at me. I wink back.

Then I cross the room to Peter and Lori's terrarium. I lift the screen off carefully and pull one out with each hand so they can coil around the bedposts while I work on their cage.

Doria would freak if she knew I let them out, even just to clean. She's convinced she'll find one of them in her toilet one morning. I told her a zillion times that it's a myth that snakes go down toilets. They're not that stupid.

When Peter and Lori are back home, I move along to Gregory and Peck, the cockatiels.

"Attagirl! Attagirl! Attagirl!" I repeat. When I bought Peck, they told me he was a talker, but so far not a word. I keep trying, though.

I let them perch on the curtain rod while I scrub. The birds are the most trouble to clean for. Some days I have to scrub the entire cage and parts of my floor. Today isn't that bad, though. I only need the steel wool for a single spot.

Robin still hasn't had her pups, but I make sure Edward G., the proud papa, is safely on his side of the cage. Daddy rats are not reliable. Last time Robin was expecting I came home from school to find her frantically searching the cage and Edward G. looking stuffed. All he left was a tiny pink tail. Robin got over it in about an hour, but my eyes still get watery when I think about those babies. They were counting on me, and I let them down.

The whole cleaning job takes about an hour and a half. I'm dropping Whoopi, Goldberg, Huckleberry, and Finn in the clean fishbowl when Al Jolson, my black-and-white cat, meows outside the window. I push it open for him, and he walks up his plank to the sill, then jumps onto the bed. "Meow-w-w-w," he wails again, and I have to go pet him. He'll keep it up till I do. He positively craves affection.

By nine o'clock, I've finished cleaning the cages, fed everybody, and washed myself. For company, I scoop Costello out of his cage and put him in my shirt pocket. Then I head for the kitchen to fix breakfast. I can tell Doria's up because there's this really disgusting smell coming from her bedroom. Sort of a cross between sweaty socks and cat pee.

I shout through her door, "Doria! Are you okay? Or are you dead and I smell your corpse rotting?"

19

"Very funny, darling," Doria calls back.

"Really, this one's *terrible*," I say to the door. "Can't you go back to the jasmine-hibiscus or whatever that was yesterday? The animals are going nuts!"

They are, too. I can hear Agnes whining and scratching at the back door, desperate to get inside and get at whatever is making that smell. It's the same way she gets when we're walking by the zoo fence. Even Costello is upset. He's climbed out of my pocket, and he's pacing back and forth across my shoulders, sniffing.

"I'm almost done, darling," Doria says. "And really, the effect is extraordinary. I don't know when I've ever felt so energized by my primal feelings!"

I ignore this. "I'm fixing breakfast. Do you want anything?"

"No, thanks. I couldn't possibly eat!"

I wouldn't think so. Whatever that stink is, it would kill anybody's appetite.

three

I'm glad Doria's room is far down the hall from the kitchen because I can't smell whatever that stuff is as I make breakfast. I'm flipping two fried eggs onto a plate when Doria comes through the door yawning and stretching. Maybe she's full of primal energy, but right now she reminds me of Rita, my lazy cat, except Doria's hair isn't orange, it's brown.

She has it pulled back with a rubber band this morning, and she's wearing a ratty old blue-and-white-striped robe thing that she bought in Greece before I was even born. Sometimes Doria comes in wearing nothing at all. One time Mr. Frank, the old guy who lives across our back fence, was out mowing his grass and he happened to glance in the window. There was Doria, stark naked, drinking a cup of tea. She waved at him. I thought he was going to drop his teeth. Doria says we should not be self-conscious about our bodies and that nature intended our skin to breathe. I say when I grow fur, I'll go naked.

"Good morning, sunshine," Doria says, and she kisses me on the cheek before she sits down across from me at the kitchen table. She still smells a little bit like whatever was coming out of her room, so I make a face. "Now, darling, how can you be bothered by my Cougar Musk? *You've* been elbow deep in rodent, reptile, and bird droppings all morning." Costello has climbed on top of my head, and Doria watches him as she says this.

"Is that what the smell was? Cougar Musk?" I ask. "No wonder Agnes was so excited."

"The Cinnamon Seminar literature calls it 'a life-affirming means of tapping into the energy of our primitive selves.' " Doria says this without even cracking a smile. When she is on one of her kicks, she gets serious. The last one was massage; before that, blue-green algae; and before that, the old movies I already mentioned.

I'm chewing, so I just nod. I am not always real patient with my mom's crazy ideas, just like she is not always real patient with my animals. But we try to get along. My dad left when I was really little, just a baby. Every month he sends a check, and there's usually a greeting card in there for me. He signs it "Love, Dad," but he doesn't write a note or anything.

"Did you get my little gift yesterday? It was Peppy Peppermint. I thought it might help with math class," she says.

"Uh, yeah. I got it. But I didn't know how to use it exactly, and uh . . . Pookie sort of made fun of it, and we had this fight and—"

"Made fun of it?" she interrupts.

"Some people don't get this Cinnamon Seminar stuff, Doria. I mean, to some people this whole idea of smells connected to feelings and all, it seems a little, uh . . . dippy."

There. I said it. And when I look up from

my yolk-and-catsup-smeared plate, Doria is smiling—thank goodness.

"They laughed at Einstein too, you know," she says.

"Einstein put Peppy Peppermint in his kid's lunch?"

This cracks us both up.

"But seriously, Rory," she begins, and she sounds all enthusiastic and sincere, like she's planning to save the whole universe. So it seems like a good time to get up from the table and clear my plate. "Cyril Cinnamon believes that different smells stimulate different parts of the brain," she says. "For example, peppermint acts directly on the learning receptors."

"Cyril Cinnamon says that, huh?" I ask.

"He's a genius, Rory. Everyone says so. That's one reason I'm so nervous about this afternoon. He's going to be here himself."

"Well, in that case Cougar Musk is not enough of a breakfast. Are you eating eggs this week?" I ask. Doria's a vegetarian, but her definition of *vegetarian* keeps changing.

Some days she only eats brown rice and tofu. Other days bacon's a vegetable too.

"Oh, no, darling, that's fine. I'll get some granola in a minute."

I know her. She'll be sitting there with her stomach growling when I come back from washing my dog. So I turn the burner back on and put a pat of butter in the frying pan. If Doria was paying attention, she'd tell me not to use butter, but eggs taste better cooked in butter, and she's nowhere near fat. In fact, for a mother, Doria doesn't look bad. She's real tall, and she has eyes as big and dark as a kangaroo rat's. She's not that wrinkled yet either.

In a few minutes I put a plate of fried eggs and toast in front of her.

"Why, darling, you're so sweet. I didn't even realize . . ."

"It's okay."

"You know, sometimes I wonder . . . ," she begins, and then we both say together, ". . . *who's the mother in this outfit!*" This is an old joke with us.

While I was cooking, Costello ran down

my arm, and now he's exploring the counter. Doria watches him while she smears marmalade on her toast.

"Costello's very clean," I say. "And besides, if he, like, *does* anything, I'll take care of it." But I cup my hand over Costello anyway and put him back in my pocket; then I tell Doria how Abby bit his ears.

"An unhappy relationship," she says. "I never bit any ears, but I know all about those. Maybe this one will be better."

" 'This one'? Which one?"

"Well, I'm sure you've noticed that Cyril—Mr. Cinnamon—and I have been seeing quite a bit of each other lately."

"Oh yeah," I answer, but really I haven't. I spend so much time with Pookie and taking care of Gerbil City and doing homework and playing soccer and all . . .

"So you've got a crush on him, huh? Or do grown-ups get crushes?"

I flop down in the chair across from her again. Is my mother's face turning pink? For some reason, that makes me feel embarrassed, so I blab something to fill the silence.

"I have a crush on a boy in my art class, sort of. His name's Sam. He has freckles."

"I guess you could say grown-ups get crushes, Rory. What's Sam like?"

Now I feel *my* face turn pink. "He's really good at soccer, the best dribbler on the team. And he's good at art. And he smiles a lot, this real crinkly silver-and-orange smile."

"Silver-and-orange?"

"He has those kind of braces that come in colors."

Maybe, if I'd thought about it, I would've figured out about Mr. Cinnamon and Doria. Sometimes when my mom gets all enthused about something, there's a man who goes with it. With the movies at the library, it was the film curator, a guy named Alfred. I liked him okay. He gave me a couple of really nice cages, and he didn't mind explaining some of the things in the movies to me. Like in *Gone With the Wind*, Scarlett O'Hara has to spend hours putting on her underwear because people a long time ago only thought women were pretty if they had these really tiny waists squeezed into really tiny lace-up underwear.

Anyway, when Alfred was in the picture, either Doria was gone or Alfred was here. At first I missed my mom, but I got used to it. Then I got real busy with my animals.

Eventually Alfred wasn't around much. Doria said they "came to a parting of the ways." Now I know that means they broke up.

"I guess that's nice, about you and Mr. Cinnamon," I say. "Even if Agnes doesn't like him."

"Agnes will learn to love him," says Doria. "Which reminds me, I have a favor to ask after you're done with her. Would you mind helping me with the seminar this afternoon? You know how fumble-fingered I get when I'm nervous, and I really want to make a good impression."

Help at the seminar? *Honestly.* I'd rather be about a zillion miles away. But it's important to her, so I say I will. "But I'm supposed to meet Pookie later," I say—almost telling the truth. "So I can only stay a little while."

She says an hour will do. I put Costello back in his cage—I don't want him to go down the drain when I'm washing Agnes—and then I come back through the kitchen to get the flea shampoo and towel from the laundry room. Doria is taking her last bite of eggs. I think of one more thing.

"You won't ever put another peppermint thing in my lunch, will you, Doria? Promise?"

four

Agnes meets me at the back door, ears alert and tail wagging. She likes her bath. Not the getting wet part but the toweling off.

"Come on, ol' girl. We'll wash you in the sink because it's so cold out. Warm water and everything."

In the garage, there's a big utility sink. I let the water run to warm up, then aim the faucet at Agnes, shielding her eyes with my hand so none will get in them. She hates having water in her eyes. Then I squeeze a dribble of shampoo onto her back and lather it into her short hair. It smells like grapefruit, something Agnes does not appreciate. First chance she gets she'll roll around in the dirt to get her own doggie smell back.

I guess Pookie is my best friend again—I'm gonna call her as soon as I'm done here—but Agnes is my next-best friend. My father brought her home before he moved away, when I was a baby and so was Agnes. We kind of grew up together. Only now we're both twelve. She's an old lady and I'm still a kid. That doesn't seem fair, but that's how it is.

I rinse Agnes, towel her off, and shoo her back in the house so she can't get dirty again. Then I go to call Pookie. As I dial, I am really glad that Pookie's parents gave her her own phone for her birthday. Her parents'll get over being mad at Agnes and me, but they probably haven't gotten over it yet. Mostly they are so busy hating each other, they don't have time to be mad at anyone else.

"Hello?"

"You sound okay," I say.

"I don't talk with my knee."

"Ha ha. How bad is it?"

"Just a couple of red marks, but she broke the skin a little. My father practically had a heart attack when he saw the blood. He wanted to know if Agnes has had her rabies shots. I told 'im she has. She has, hasn't she?"

"Of course! They won't even give you a dog license unless the dog's had all the shots. I'm really really sorry," I say. "Agnes didn't mean it."

"I always thought she liked me."

"She does. But you scared her when you ran at me like that. I don't think her eyes are that great anymore. Are you grounded?" I ask.

"I don't think so. Mom asked me to watch Barney this afternoon. She and Dad have to go to a counselor or something. I thought I'd take him to the zoo."

"Can I come along?"

"Sure . . . only . . ."

"Only what?"

"Well, my parents don't want me to see you. Mom said you're a bad influence."

"Why? Because I was outside your house at night?"

"That. And you 'lured me' outside. That's what my dad said. And . . . well, I don't think they're too crazy about Doria."

I consider for a second. "Look, Pookie, I know Doria's pretty different from your mom and all . . ."

"Yeah. My mom doesn't sell stink bombs. Hey—Stink Bomb Mom. It rhymes." She cracks up.

This makes me mad. "At least she doesn't kick dogs!"

"Golly molly, Rory. I *know*. Dad's just awful lately. I think it's because of him and Mom. . . . Is Agnes okay?"

"She's a tough old girl."

There's another pause. I'm not sure whether we're having a fight now or not. Pookie must be thinking the same thing. "I don't want to fight with you, Rory. I get plenty of fighting around here. I'd say my mom and dad are just stuck with you. Best friends?"

"Best friends," I confirm. "So what if I just happen to be at the zoo? At two o'clock?"

"Meet you by the reptile house."

Just as Pookie hangs up, Agnes starts barking, and a second later I hear the doorbell ring. Oh gosh, I didn't realize it was that late. The next sound is the door opening and Doria's voice: "Welcome to Cinnamon Seminars!"

33

five

When I realize it's time for the Cinnamon Seminar, my first thought is: Hide!

So I duck into my bedroom. The animals seem excited. W.C., a guinea pig grandchild, and Cooper, one of the hamsters, are exercising furiously on their wheels, which squeak and whirr. Al Jolson is pacing back and forth on the windowsill, and Cassidy, my rabbit, is doing her whirling dervish trick—spinning around and thumping her hind legs to get my attention. *Thumpa-thumpa-thumpa-thumpa* clockwise, *thumpa-thumpa-thumpa-thumpa* counterclockwise.

It must be the seminar that has everybody so revved up. A few mystery smells have

34

already drifted in, some good and some bad. I guess Doria is getting ready.

Agnes click-clicks in to lie down on her pillow and falls asleep instantly. I haven't spritzed Margaret today. Iguanas like to be spritzed with a squirt bottle a couple of times every day so they don't dry out. Margaret looks up sleepily when I do this, not a bit grateful.

"Attagirl. Attagirl. Attagirl?" I say hopefully to Peck. He just blinks at me.

There must be some other job I need to do. Only I can't think of what it is.

"Rory?" I hear Doria call. I guess it's time to get it over with.

In the living room, Doria is pushing chairs around so they face a card table set up by the door into the dining room. She has changed out of the ratty robe thing and brushed her hair. She's wearing a long orange-and-blue skirt and a lavender T-shirt. This is dressed up for Doria.

"*There* you are," she says to me in that supercheerful voice kindergarten teachers use. I can't figure out why she's talking that way, but then Mr. Cinnamon comes

35

through the doorway carrying two pitchers full of water. He must've been who was at the front door.

Mr. Cinnamon is very tall, the tallest man I've ever seen outside a circus, so tall he has to tilt his head to get through a regular-size door. He is also skinny, and on his head is a heap of hair that reminds me of a Raggedy Ann doll's after you've tried to comb it. He wears that kind of glasses that have only half a piece of glass for each eye, and he always wears a tie and a white shirt. Today the tie is green.

Doria said he was handsome. I say she must really like him a lot to think so.

"Cyril," she says, "you've met my daughter, Aurora?"

"Why yes, of course," says Mr. Cinnamon. "How are your nostrils today, my dear? Ready for their very first Cinnamon Seminar?"

"I guess so," I say. "How are yours?"

"Tip-top, my dear, as always. Doria, I wonder if you and Aurora might not want to move that sofa? So that the guests can see the demonstration better?"

The sofa is heavy, and Doria and I have to heave-ho to get it where he's pointing.

"Hmmmm," he says. "No, I don't think so. Back a little bit, perhaps?"

Doria and I manage to slide it a few inches back. But he doesn't like that either.

"You might want to put the pitchers down and help, Cyril," says Doria. She is breathing hard.

"Well, I would," he says, "but my back, you know. And this morning I stubbed my toe in the shower."

"I think the sofa is just fine here," Doria says. Mr. Cinnamon looks like he's going to make another suggestion, but Doria raises her eyebrows at him, and he doesn't.

"What do you want me to do, Doria?" I ask. She tells me to get a fan from the hall closet and put it on the floor aimed at the card table. I have no idea why I'm doing this, but I do, and I'm just putting the plug in the wall when the doorbell rings.

"Oh my goodness," says Doria. "That must be the first guests. Go get the door, Rory."

"Remember to say 'Welcome to Cinnamon Seminars!' " Mr. Cinnamon calls at me.

I turn the knob, wishing like mad I didn't have to say such a dumb thing, especially to a total stranger. But when I see who it is at the door I'm so surprised I can't say anything at all. I just stand there with my mouth open like a gasping fish.

"Well, Rory Mudd! How nice. I didn't realize this was your home," says Mr. Goode, the principal of my school, who is standing on our front step.

"Welcome," I manage to say, "welcome to . . ." Then I get stuck again. "Mr. Goode, you're not here for . . . ?"

"The seminar. Why, yes I am, Rory. May I come in?"

"I guess so," I say, moving out of his way. Then I realize maybe this doesn't sound very polite. "Welcome to Cinnamon Seminars," I say at last, but Mr. Goode is already in the front hall, and Doria is offering to take his coat. A couple of women are coming up our walk, a man's getting out of a blue car parked at the curb, and a big white car is pulling into our driveway.

Then I get the second shock of the past thirty seconds.

The white car is as long as my house and so clean and waxed and polished it positively glows. I only know one car on the whole planet like that. It's Gramma!

"Welcome to Cinnamon Seminars!" I say to the two women, and "Welcome to Cinnamon Seminars!" I say to the man from the blue car.

Gramma is right behind him. "Welcome to Cinnamon Seminars!" I say to her too. She smiles and gives me a hug. "What are you doing here?" I whisper in her ear.

My grandmother, Doria's mother, is short like me, but she stands very straight, so she looks taller. Today she is wearing a light blue skirt and jacket and black high heels that match the purse that's over her arm. She has the kind of thin white hair that old ladies have if they have been going to the beauty parlor every week for practically their entire lives. I think she must've gone there this morning too, because she smells poison-sweet—like hairspray.

"I just thought I ought to see what your

mother's gotten herself into now," Gramma replies. "What do you know about it, sweetheart? Perfume or cologne or something?"

"Something like that," I say. I don't know how I'd ever explain Cinnamon Seminars to Gramma. "Does Doria know you're coming?" I ask.

"You shouldn't call your mother by her first name, dear. It doesn't show proper respect," says Gramma. "No, she doesn't know. I thought I'd surprise her."

A few more people are coming up the walk, so I step aside and let Gramma in. I bet Doria—I mean my mother—will be surprised all right.

When there are no more guests, I go back to the living room. If Doria is in shock because of Gramma, it doesn't show on her face. Maybe Cougar Musk works after all.

Doria motions me to stand next to her at the table. It's set up with beakers like the ones we use for science, pitchers of water, and little squirt bottles like the one I squirt Margaret with. In the middle of it all is a purple case that says CINNAMON SEMINARS on

40

it in big red letters. It is pretty embarrassing to be standing here in front of all these people.

I count the "guests," fourteen of them. Cyril Cinnamon is sitting in our most comfortable chair, the one Al Jolson usually curls up in. Gramma is sitting in a chair next to him with her purse in her lap and her hands folded over it. Mr. Goode is on the sofa next to a dark-haired woman wearing blue jeans and a yellow T-shirt covered with pictures of pink pigs. He smiles at me, and I try to smile back.

I've been so busy saying "Welcome welcome welcome" and wondering about Gramma showing up that I haven't really thought about how weird it is that the principal of my school is actually at my house. It's even weirder that he's at my house for something as absolutely dumb as a Cinnamon Seminar.

"My name is Doria Capehart," says my mother, "and I'll be your Olfactory Guide this afternoon. Before we begin, there is a very important person I'd like you to meet."

I'm terrified that the person is going to be

me, but it turns out to be Mr. Cinnamon, who waves to the other people just like a princess on a parade float. Everybody claps except Gramma.

"Now, as you know," says Doria, "Cinnamon Seminar Plan A was invented by Mr. Cinnamon himself in association with Far Eastern monks and top scientists. We guarantee you five degrees of personal growth in only three weeks, or your money back."

I don't know what she's talking about, but everybody looks real interested.

"Many people find they are so delighted with Cinnamon Seminars that they wish to purchase Plan B as well," Doria says. "This week only, if you purchase both Plans A and B, I am able to offer you a five percent discount!"

My grandmother raises her hand.

Doria takes a deep breath, then says, "Yes?" and nods at her.

"Doria, dear, just what exactly *is* Cinnamon Seminars?"

Doria takes another deep breath. "I'm glad you asked that question," she says. I'm kind of proud that she isn't letting herself get rattled. Usually my grandmother drives her absolutely crazy. "I think the best way to explain our all-natural product is to experience it. Rory, would you open the case and remove the blue package with the marbles in it, please?"

I feel sort of like the blond lady on that TV game show as I open the package and pull out six plastic marble things, then drop each in a different beaker of water the way Doria asks me to. As the plastic part of the marbles dissolves, a salty smell fills the room.

"Aaaaaaaaaaaaaaaaaah," says the lady sitting next to Mr. Goode. He gives her a funny look and scoots the other way on the couch.

"We're starting with the easier aromas," Doria says, "the ones most of us appreciate immediately. Now breathe deeply. Can anyone identify the aroma?"

"The ocean!" Mr. Goode says. "The beach!" says a lady who has fluffy hair just like Pookie's mom's.

"Good!" says Doria. "You are a very sensitive group. This is Essence of Sea Spray.

Like all our aromas, it's made only from natural ingredients. Breathe deeply, close your eyes, and feel the power of the aroma. Try to experience the sounds of the sea birds, the roar of the ocean, the warmth of the sunshine . . ."

I close my eyes and try to do what Doria says, but all I can think of is rotting fish. I wonder what "natural ingredients" go into those little marbles anyway.

"Would anyone like to share what they're feeling?" Doria asks.

"I feel at peace with myself," says the lady with the fluffy hair.

"I feel in harmony with the universe," says the lady sitting next to Mr. Goode.

"I feel seasick," says Mr. Goode.

Doria is saying, "Wonderful, wonderful" until Mr. Goode speaks. Then she says, "Oh dear, do you need . . . ?"

"No, no, I'll be okay," he says. "Ever since I was in the navy I've had a little trouble with the ocean is all."

"Let's try another one," Doria says quickly. "Rory, will you switch on the fan to clear the room? Rory is my assistant, ladies and gentlemen."

"*And* your daughter," Gramma pipes up as the fan begins to hum.

"And this is my mother," Doria says.

"Quite the little family affair today, isn't it?" Mr. Cinnamon says, and the "guests" laugh politely.

"We'll use the atomizers this time while we allow the Sea Spray aroma to fade," says Doria.

The atomizers are the little squirt bottles. Doria explained that to me the day I caught her spraying Al Jolson. I was going to get mad, but then I realized Al Jolson was purring.

"Catnip," Doria said.

Now Doria takes three atomizers from the table and hands them around. "Please spray your face and then pass it to your neighbor," she says.

The big question is, Will Gramma squirt?

The lady on the floor next to her inhales a big whiff, sighs happily, then passes the atomizer to Gramma. She takes it and looks at it the way she'd look at a bug in her under-wear drawer.

"Go ahead, Mother," says Doria.

"My mascara will run," Gramma says.

"As a matter of fact, it won't," says Mr. Cinnamon. "Cinnamon Seminar atomizers exude such a fine mist that makeup is not affected."

Now the room is quiet and everyone is looking at Gramma.

"Be a sport, Mama," somebody says.

Trapped, she closes her eyes tight and presses the squirter for about a tenth of a second.

Then she hands the atomizer to the next person and gets a tissue out of her purse to wipe her face.

"There. Now that wasn't so bad, was it?" says Mr. Cinnamon.

Gramma glares at him.

Finally the atomizer gets to me. I point the little hole right at my nose, close my eyes, and squirt. This is a good one. Choco-late.

"Does anyone wish to share?" Doria asks.

"I feel warm and content."

"I feel the innocence of childhood."

The innocence of childhood. *Honestly.*

"I feel hungry," says Mr. Goode, and everybody laughs.

It's twenty to two, and I'm supposed to meet Pookie. Doria is doing real well, so I decide I'll only stay for one more smell. I'm hoping it's another good one, like bubble gum or popcorn.

"This aroma is a bit more challenging," says Doria. "But I think this group is ready for it. I can sense how you hunger for experience." She motions for me to click off the fan while she rummages around in the bag and pulls out a package of marbles full of yellow liquid. She's got the package half open when she looks down at the label and changes her mind.

"Ooops, wrong one," she says, and for the first time she looks flustered.

"Need some help, Doria?" Mr. Cinnamon asks.

"We've got it, Cyril," she says. "Rory," she whispers. "Look in the case down on the floor and pull out the package with the gold marbles in it. They're a little darker than these lemon ones."

The package she wants is right on top, and I hand it to her. There's something about having all those eyes on us, waiting, that makes me really want to hurry, so I don't even look at the label.

Doria rips open the package and drops the marbles into a beaker of water. The stuff works fast, and in a second I see faces screw up like a skunk just did its business.

Yuck. Sweaty socks and cat pee. It has to be Cougar Musk.

I'm just edging toward the door, hoping I can get out of the room fast, when I hear something. A high-pitched crying sound— "Arrrh-arrh-arrh"—sort of like a seal barking.

I've never heard her make a noise like this before, but I realize what it is.

Agnes!

The door to my room is open. There's nothing to stop her from running in here and going after . . . what? The air? Everybody?

48

I start for the doorway to head her off, but I'm too late. I can already hear her toenails click-clicking down the hall. As soon as she reaches the living room she starts barking and howling like crazy. She whizzes past before I can catch her—right into the Cinnamon Seminar.

"Watch out!" I yell.

The people sitting on the floor jump up and scatter like popcorn, which is really pretty funny because Agnes is only about as tall as a footstool. I mean, she's no rottweiler. Even so, Mr. Cinnamon has actually jumped up on his chair.

"Agnes, Agnes! C'mere, puppy, that's a *good* puppy," hollers Doria, adding to the noise.

Gramma is trying a different strategy. She's down on the floor, looking very un-Gramma-like, holding out her hand and calling softly, "Aggie dear, come to Gramma, Aggie dear. It's all *right*. . . ."

Gramma is usually very dignified, but she does like dogs.

"Come on, ol' girl," I say, moving toward Agnes slowly.

Suddenly Agnes goes nuts. She jumps in the air and twirls around and around and around—snapping her jaws the way she does when she's trying to catch flies.

This scares Mr. Cinnamon so much he vaults over the back of his chair and maneuvers it in front of him like a shield.

"I'm so sorry about all this," Doria calls out, trying to make herself heard over Agnes. I think my mom has just noticed that most of her customers are backed against the furniture looking terrified. Only Mr. Goode has stayed in his seat, and he's smiling like he's watching something funny on TV.

"She's really not a vicious dog," Doria continues. "It's just the aroma . . . yes, a visible demonstration of the power of the aroma. . . ."

"Do you . . . do you think . . . is it safe to move, do you think?" asks the lady in the T-shirt with the pigs. "As a child, I had a traumatic experience with a dog . . . and . . . I think I'd better go now."

Agnes quiets down when she hears this voice. She's just standing there, cocking her head and flapping her batwing ears like she doesn't know what to do next. Finally she lies down and covers her nose with her paws.

"Oh dear, but you can't possibly leave yet!" Doria is saying. "I have order forms, and this week I'm offering a five percent discount. . . ." But most of the people are gathering their coats.

I'm thinking it's a good time to make my exit too. I have a feeling I'm in trouble, even though none of this is my fault. It certainly wasn't my idea to give everybody a blast of Cougar Musk. "Gotta go, Doria." I'm heading for the door. "See ya!"

"Wait one minute, Aurora," she says.

Mr. Cinnamon is the first one out. He looks shaky and white and forgets to duck his head when he gets to the front door, so—*thwack*—he gets a good one right in the middle of his forehead.

"Cyril . . . ?" Doria calls after him, but he just raises his hand, whatever that means, and keeps going.

I go back in the living room and put the marbles away in their packages, and the packages in the bags. The Cougar Musk marbles look almost exactly like the lemon ones, and I hope I'm getting them put back in the right places.

By the time I'm done, everyone is gone except for Gramma and Mr. Goode. Gramma has turned on the fan to clear out the smell, and now she's petting Agnes.

I can't figure out why Mr. Goode is still hanging around, but it turns out he actually wants to place an order.

"A case of the chocolate spray," he says to Doria. Then he winks at me. "For the kindergartners."

I do my best to smile back. Mr. Goode is an okay guy—for a principal.

"I'm so terribly sorry about how this all ended up," says Doria as she fills out the order form.

"Think nothing of it," says Mr. Goode. "We can't expect dogs to have the same, uh, what's the right word . . . appreciation? of smells that we humans have."

Actually, dogs have a much *greater* appreciation of smells than humans have, and that's what caused the trouble. But I don't say anything.

Doria hands back the receipt for the order, but Mr. Goode doesn't make any move to leave. For some reason, I remember that he's divorced, like my mother. And he's about her age too.

"Thank you for coming," says Doria after a pause. She holds out her hand, and he takes it.

"When do I pick up the chocolate spray?" he asks before he finally lets go of her hand.

"It should be ready next week," Doria says. "I'll give you a call."

Mr. Goode backs out the front door still smiling at Doria, and almost trips when he gets to the step. I am thinking two things: One, I wish he'd stay long enough for Doria to forget she's going to yell at me, and two, he would be a *big* improvement over Mr. Cinnamon.

"I'm late to meet Pookie," I say when the door clicks shut.

Doria turns to face me. "Your dog ruined

my Cinnamon Seminar!'' she says. "And did you see the way Cyril ran out of here? He'll never speak to me again!''

I really am sorry the seminar got wrecked, even though it wasn't Agnes's fault. And I'd probably even apologize. But now I'm mad. Mr. Cinnamon is such a dweeb.

"My dog was being a dog!" I say. "And anyway, Cougar Musk is stupid. Mr. Cinnamon is stupid if you ask me. Why do you get mixed up with that stuff anyway? Why can't you sell Tupperware or makeup like other people's mothers?''

Doria starts to cry. "Oh, what's the use? You're just like your father. You'll never understand anything . . ."

"What!" I say. The only time she ever brings up my father is when his monthly check is due.

"You remind me of him more every day. Always practical. Never any imagination. Never willing to try anything new."

"Well, what if I am like him?" I say. "At least he works! At least he helps people with something practical—like cutting them open and taking out the sick parts."

"Oh yes, the great doctor! And how did he help us anyway?" Doria says. "Walked out before you were even a year old."

If Doria's plan is to make me cry too, she's doing a good job. I don't think about my dad much. What's the point? But it hasn't exactly escaped my notice that most of my friends have fathers and, except for monthly greeting cards, I don't.

But I'm not going to start blubbering, no matter what Doria says.

And now help arrives.

"What are you two carrying on about?" Gramma says. She is standing in the doorway between the living room and the entry hall.

"Stay out of this, Mother," says Doria.

"I will not," says Gramma. "You're being too hard on the child. Seems to me a little practicality wouldn't hurt this household. And don't tell me you've got some romantic attachment to that tall redheaded fellow, Doria? Hazelnut or whatever his name was? Have my daughter's standards dipped that low?"

"That's it. Gang up on me!" Doria says.

"My new job's in ruins. My love life's in ruins. And now you two are in cahoots against me too. Well, what do I expect? I never could do anything right. It's the story of my life."

Doria turns her back to us and stalks down the hall toward her bedroom. My grandmother and I look at each other. Then, from behind the chair in the living room, comes a long mournful howl.

six

"So do you think it's true?" Pookie asks. "That you're like your dad?"

We're sharing a bag of peanuts and watching the dromedaries chew alfalfa. Barney is running in circles around us. Every once in a while he comes over, grabs a peanut out of the bag, then runs off again.

"It would explain a lot if you were," Pookie says. "Like how come you and Doria don't get along so well lately. And how come she's a nutcase and you're not."

"Pookie!"

"Okay, so that wasn't exactly polite. But you're my best friend so I can tell you what I really think. You know, you *could* go live with your dad. He's a doctor, right? And he

57

lives in a big house and sends loads of money every month. So probably it would be great. Have you ever thought of that?"

"When I was little I used to think about going to live with him sometimes," I say. "But I've hardly talked to him the last couple of years—only on my birthday and Christmas. It's like he's too busy even to call me."

"He'd have to say yes if you asked him," Pookie says. "Wouldn't he?"

I don't say anything, just watch the dromedaries. I wonder if there's alfalfa in the Arabian desert.

"Meow meow meow!" Barney sings as he runs toward us. He holds out his hand, Pookie hands him a handful of peanuts, and he runs off again, crunching on them.

Pookie says something about Barney, but I'm not listening. What would it be like to live with my dad—somebody who isn't *embarrassing* like Doria?

"Aurora Mudd!"

"Sorry. What?"

"I asked what kind of people go to these Cinnamon things anyway?"

"Oh my gosh, I can't believe I forgot to tell you!" I say. "You'd never guess in a zillion years. Mr. Goode was there!"

"Get outta here!"

"I swear! I was *so* embarrassed. The weird thing was, I kind of got the feeling he likes Doria."

"You mean likes or *likes*?" Pookie asks.

"You know, *likes*, but grown-ups are so weird it's hard to tell."

"Another reason to go live with your dad. It'd be like teacher's pet if she married him, only worse."

I feel around the salt at the bottom of the bag for the last peanut. "Want another one, Barney . . . Barney?" I look around, and don't see him. "Where'd he go?"

"Golly molly, not *again!*" Pookie moans.

One thing about taking Barney anyplace, you've got to watch him every second. His legs are short, but he can really move. Kind of like Agnes.

He's already disappeared once today, before I got here. Pookie was putting mustard on the hot dogs; she went to hand him his, and he was gone. Like always, though, he was easy to find. He loves the big cats.

I turn in a slow circle, scanning the area like a light in a lighthouse. No Barney.

"You go right, and I'll go left," says Pookie. "We'll meet at the cougars in fifteen minutes. He'll be over by the cats somewhere, unless he got lost on the way."

Pookie has looking for Barney down to a system.

I carry out my assignment, walking quickly with my hands in my back pockets to keep them warm. "Barney!" I yell about once a minute.

I walk past the sloth bear, who is curled in a ball in a corner of his cage sleeping—I wish I had his shaggy coat—and the giraffes, who make me think of Mr. Cinnamon.

When I round the curve by the spider monkeys I can see where they keep the cats. In front of what used to be the lion cage is a bulldozer, a wheelbarrow, stacks of lumber, and a pile of sand. I remember Pookie told me they're building new houses for some of the zoo animals, "habitats" they call them.

It looks like the lions have just moved into their new place, but the wall that separates people from animals isn't done yet. About half of it is just wire fence. Yellow plastic ribbon is strung around on sawhorses to keep people away until the work's done. Of course, on Saturday, the construction guys aren't here.

"Barney!" I yell.

"Petta ki'y! Petta ki'y!"

Thank goodness! That's him. He's trying to say "pet the kitty." He doesn't talk that good yet.

"Where are you?"

I duck under the ribbon, wondering what somebody who saw me would think. Probably figure I'm some kind of crazy person trying to climb in with the lions.

"Barney?"

"Ni-i-i-ice ki'y! C'mere, ki'y!"

On the other side of the sand pile I spot him—halfway up the fence! Barney's quite a climber, the best in his preschool, Pookie says. The two lions on the other side are watching him.

"Get down from there right now! They're dangerous!" I yell. I am in a panic, running toward him.

Barney is grinning from ear to ear. "Hi, Wohwee. See a ki'y? Bi-i-i-i-ig ki'y."

I get my hands on him finally and yank him down, not too gently. Now that he's safe he starts to howl.

"Petta ki'y! Petta ki'y!"

"No!" I say. "Kitty too big! Kitty eat you all up!"

For some reason he thinks this is hilarious, and he starts to laugh. "Ki'y eat Ba'ney all up!"

"That's right," I say. "No more Barney."

This makes him laugh even harder. "No mo' Ba'ney! No mo' Ba'ney!"

I carry him back toward the cougars to meet Pookie. He's soft, warm, and heavy in my arms, and even though Pookie thinks he's a royal pain, I have to admit I think he's cute. He's got hair so blond it's almost white, and twinkly blue eyes and big pink cheeks. He's practically always smiling.

Pookie shakes her head and comes striding toward us looking just exactly like her father did last night in front of their house.

"Bernard Tunnbaum!" she says. "Don't you ever ever ever ever ever—"

"Big ki'y eat Ba'ney all up!" he says happily. "No mo' Ba'ney!" He laughs and laughs.

"No kidding, Pook," I say. "He was halfway into the lions' cage. Climbing right up the fence. Scared me half to death."

"Golly molly!" Her eyes get big. "Think how much trouble I'd be in if the lions ate him!"

Then she grins like she didn't mean it. "Come on, Tiger," she says, and holds out her arms. "We better get outta here." She bares her teeth and growls, "Rrrrrrrrrr," until he laughs so hard he doubles over in her arms.

seven

Twenty minutes later I walk in the front door, and Agnes barks hello like this afternoon never happened.

Doria says dogs are dumb, but I say dogs have really short memories.

Except about food.

While I was walking home I was all excited about saving Barney from the lions, but now that I'm here it doesn't seem like any big deal. He probably couldn't have gotten into the lions' house anyway.

I go in the bedroom to check Robin, and while I'm there I look in on Peck. "Attagirl! Attagirl! Attagirl!" I say. He opens his beak, but there's no sound. Maybe I should try "Polly wanna cracker."

In the kitchen I get Agnes a cup of kibble for her dinner. Then I get out the cheese to make myself a sandwich. There are a couple of notes on the refrigerator door.

Aurora, dear—
Please call me if you need or want any-
thing. Don't worry about the little tiff this
afternoon. Things will be fine.

Love,
Your Grandmother

And the second one:

Ro—
At lib. ptlk. Bak late.

Do

Doria still volunteers at the library twice a week, even though she doesn't catalog movies anymore. While I grate cheese for my sandwich, I wonder what she brought to the potluck. Essence of Sea Spray?

I can't think of anything I need or want from Gramma, but after I eat my grilled cheese sandwich I call her anyway. Pop answers the phone, but the news is on TV so he hands it off to Gramma after a quick "How are you?" Gramma asks if I've done my homework—I have—and I tell her about rescuing Barney from the lions.

"You're a hero!" she says.

"Aw, Gramma."

"Well, I'm proud of you."

Gramma asks about Agnes, and I say she's recovered from the excitement this afternoon.

"You know, dear," Gramma says, "there's some truth in what your mother was saying today."

"About what?"

"About you and your father. You remind me of him. Whatever he did to your mother, he has supported you all these years—with a little help from Pop and me."

"It's weird to be like somebody I barely even know," I say.

"The divorce was hard on both of them. I don't think Doria will ever forgive him, but maybe someday you can."

"Gramma," I say, trying to think of a way

66

to bring this up. "What would you think
. . . what do you think Doria would say if I
wanted to go live . . ."

"Go live with your father?"

"Yeah."

"Has your father invited you?"

"Not exactly," I say. But I am thinking
Pookie is right. He'd *have* to say yes if I
asked him. Wouldn't he?

"I guess I'd say that's up to you and your
father . . . and your mother, of course.
Are you unhappy, dear?"

"It's just that lately, everything Doria—I
mean my mother—does is so embarrassing."

There's a silence; then I hear my grandmother sigh. "When your mother was your
age, she thought I was the most embarrassing person who ever lived. Of course, Pop
and I weren't divorced so she was stuck with
us. Now that you mention it, she *still* thinks
we're embarrassing."

"But at least you didn't sell stink
bombs—I mean, Cinnamon Seminars."

"Different things embarrass different
people, I guess," Gramma says. "Which re-

minds me, is she really involved with that con man? Hazelnut or whatever it was?"

"Looks like it."

"Oh, my *word*. Rory, promise me you'll show more sense about men than your mother has. You're not even interested in boys yet, are you?"

"I'm more interested in other things—like my animals," I say.

"Good girl," Gramma says. "Plenty of time for all that other later on."

We talk a few more minutes. "Sweet dreams," she says before she hangs up.

While I'm refilling food dishes and water bottles, I think about Gramma. I can see why she might have embarrassed Doria when she was young, and why she drives Doria crazy now. She is pretty nosy, and she always knows what's best—even when she doesn't.

But still. I'm glad there was somebody around tonight to wish me sweet dreams.

eight

Tuesday after school I check the water dishes in Gerbil City and make sure Robin's okay. Then I head to the kitchen for a snack.

Doria isn't home—this is her day for yoga. Since the seminar on Saturday, we've communicated mostly by notes on the refrigerator. You'd think by now she'd've forgiven me—especially since Mr. Cinnamon came creeping back the very next day.

He had a big purple bruise on his forehead from where he thwacked his head on the door. And he made Doria lock Agnes in my room before he would come in the house. *Honestly.*

Agnes greeted me at the door and now she's running along beside me, barking like a puppy. The thing about dogs is, first, if they like you, they like you a lot, and second, if they like you, they like you forever.

I get the yogurt out of the refrigerator, put a big gob in a bowl, add honey and applesauce, and stir it all around. Then I give Agnes a cinnamon graham cracker and she trots off to eat it in the corner.

The mail is in a pile on the table, and when I sit down to eat I look through it.

My dad's monthly envelope is there, addressed to Ms. Doria Capehart and Ms. Aurora Mudd, like always. Besides the check, which I stick on the refrigerator, there's the usual card. This month's has a photograph of three kittens in a basket, and inside, it says, "Wishing you a warm, fuzzy day." He signed it, "Love, Dad."

I wish there was a note or something. Maybe he could tell me what kind of surgery he did that day, or even what he ate for breakfast. Mayor Tunnbaum may be a creep, but at least Pookie knows what he eats for breakfast—cornflakes with fake sugar, the kind that comes in those pink packets. Practically the only thing I know about my dad is that he has tiny handwriting.

I look at the card again. Those kittens aren't having a warm, fuzzy day at all. I bet the camera scared them.

I flip through the rest of the mail, and I'm really surprised to find a long white envelope with "Ms. Aurora Mudd" typed on it.

Right away, I have a bad feeling about this envelope. I don't even want to open it. Then I see the return address, and I *really* don't want to open it. It's from the Municipal Court, County of Catamount.

What does the Municipal Court want with me? I'm just a kid!

I finish my yogurt and wash out the dish; then I go in my room and get Peter out of his terrarium. Reptiles like to snuggle up to warm-blooded creatures, and having a snake draped over my shoulder makes me feel more confident about opening this letter.

I sit back down and tear open the envelope. Inside is a letter on white paper. At the top of the page is a blue picture of a snarling wildcat's head, and underneath that in shiny gold letters it says "County of Catamount." It looks official and scary.

Dear Ms. Mudd:

According to the records of the Department of Animal Control, County of Catamount, you are the owner of a female mongrel dog, color brown, licensed under the name ''Agnes.''

It is our regrettable duty to inform you as owner of said brown female dog that, pursuant to complaints by a citizen of the County of Catamount, she has been declared a vicious animal.

Said complaints have been substantiated by the Municipal Court and the Office of the Mayor. You therefore have no recourse available to you.

You are hereby ordered to surrender the female mongrel dog, ''Agnes,'' to officers of the Department of Animal Control who will visit your home for

this purpose between 4 p.m. and 5 p.m.
on Thursday, October 8.

Sincerely,

John Catspaw
John Catspaw
Clerk of the Court

There are a lot of big words in that letter, but not so many that I don't get the idea. Somebody told somebody Agnes is dangerous, and now the police are gonna put her in jail.

I am practically in shock. How long does Agnes have to stay in jail? Where is the jail? How often can I visit her? Will they give her a bath every week?

And then something even more terrible occurs to me.

What if they aren't going to put her in jail at all?

What if they're going to put her to sleep?

Right at this moment, Agnes comes trotting over—*clickety-click, clickety-click*—and puts her head in my lap to be petted.

A big tear gets loose from my eye and rolls down my cheek. Agnes is *my* dog. My second-best friend. She's *old*. Who would ever call her vicious?

Somebody at the Cinnamon Seminar? But all she did was bark. If the cops rounded up every barking dog, they wouldn't have time to do anything else.

I read the letter again. And it hits me.

"Office of the Mayor," it says. That means Mr. Tunnbaum.

I'm so upset about the letter, I don't even hear the putt-putt of the VW van or the squeak of the garage door. But now the back door opens, and in walks my mother.

From the way her eyes narrow I can tell she's about to yell at me for having the snake out. But then she realizes I'm crying.

"Rory, darling, whatever's happened?"

nine

I am crying the way I used to sometimes when I was little—so hard that I can't even talk and I can't even stop and my whole body is shaking.

Agnes licks my leg, Peter clings a little tighter, and Doria's mouth drops open in surprise.

I hand over Mr. Catspaw's letter, and Doria starts to read. Through my tears, she looks all blurry.

"This is terrible!" Doria says when she's done reading. "But what's it about, anyway? Agnes, vicious? It's too ridiculous."

I tell her about the night Agnes bit Pookie. "But even Pookie said it was no big deal!"

"Well, that explains that anyway," Doria says.

"Explains what?"

" 'No recourse,' " Doria says. "That means there's nothing you can do about it because the decision has already been made. In ordinary circumstances, there would probably have to be a hearing or something. A chance for you to defend your dog."

"But why isn't this ordinary?" I ask.

"Because Agnes picked the wrong person to nip—Mayor Tunnbaum's daughter."

"But can't you do anything?" I feel like I'm going to start crying again.

Doria doesn't say anything, just looks down at the letter. But I can see by the way her mouth has gotten pursed up that she's mad.

"Who does he think he is anyway?" she says. "First I'll call my friend Chris down at the newspaper. Then I'll call Annie at the TV station. If they won't help, I'll see who I can get to sit in at his office with me."

"Doria—" I start to say, but I can't get a word in.

"He can't do this to you!" she says. "It's

unjust! I'm sure I can get the Humane Society to picket City Hall. I'll picket his house myself."

"Mom!"

"Get me the phone book, darling."

Doria sounds the same way she does when she talks about Cinnamon Seminars—all enthusiastic and sincere. Suddenly I have a bad feeling about getting her help.

"Maybe you could just *talk* to him?" I say.

Doria stands up and reaches out to hug me, but Peter flicks his tongue to see what's coming, and she pulls back.

"I'll put him away," I say. "Don't, like, do anything or go anywhere."

Once Peter's under the bed, I come back to the kitchen, where Doria is now pacing and muttering to herself.

"I'm practicing what I'm going to say to that old fascist—I mean, Mayor Bernard Tunnbaum," she explains. Her hand's on the doorknob.

"Mom . . . uh, do you think you could put on regular clothes?"

Doria looks down at herself. She's still

wearing the purple leotard and tie-dyed sweats she always wears to yoga. I'm pretty mortified if she even goes to the grocery store like that.

"What do you suggest I wear?" she asks.

"Well, a skirt maybe. And—do you own any nylons?"

Five minutes later, Doria comes out wearing a black skirt, a red-and-white-striped sweater, and dark green tights.

"Okay?" she says.

"Okay," I reply, but I am thinking—for about the zillionth time—that she *must* be color-blind. "Good luck," I say to the door as it closes behind her.

ten

I f I just sit here I'll go crazy worrying about Agnes.

Edward G. needs a cage for after the pups come, and the pet store doesn't close till seven, so I decide I'll go get him one.

My savings are in an old gym sock in my underwear drawer—piggy banks are so *dumb*, why not just *tell* the robbers where you keep your money?—so I get out fifteen dollars, enough for a small cage, plus a little extra to buy pinkies for the snakes and a box of puppy treats.

"Come on, Agnes," I call.

She tugs toward the zoo when we get to the sidewalk, but the pet shop's the other way, so I have to pull her along. I think about walking by Pookie's house, see if it's rumbling or anything, but I don't. I try not to think about it.

Outside Suzy's Pet Barn, I wind Agnes's leash around a parking meter and tell her to stay.

The swinging door is connected up with one of those cylinder toys that flip over and make a noise, so when I walk in there's this loud *meeee-oooowwwww.*

"How's my best customer?" Suzy asks. She's standing at the cash register writing something on a clipboard. There's nobody else in the store, and it's quiet—except for the gurgling of the fishtanks in back and an occasional screech from one of the parrots.

I don't feel like talking about the disaster with Agnes so I just say I'm fine except for needing a rat cage.

"You know where they are," she says without looking up. "We got some new Habitrails in this week. Check 'em out."

The cages are in the back so I don't see who it is when the "cat" announces the door again.

"Back wall," I hear Suzy say.

In a moment there are sneaker-steps padding back to where I'm trying to decide between splurging on a new Habitrail or just getting a plain ol' wire cage. When I look over my shoulder, there's Sam, the boy with the freckles in my art class, the one I almost have a crush on.

"Hi, Rory," he says, and flashes me his orange-and-silver smile.

"You have rodents too?" I ask. It's a stupid question. Obviously he has rodents or he wouldn't be looking at rodent cages.

But he says no. "We live in an apartment so I've never had a pet. Now my mom says I can have a rat. If I save up enough to buy a cage, she'll buy 'im for me. So I wanted to find out how much cages cost."

"That's a good deal for your mom. The rat's practically free. The cages cost more. You can build one yourself, though, if you want. It's pretty easy."

"Have you ever built a cage?" Now he seems sort of impressed.

"Yeah, sure." Would he think I was really weird if he knew about Gerbil City?

"Maybe you could . . . uh . . . help

me," he says. "After school or something. These look pretty expensive."

I like the way there are a whole bunch of freckles on his nose, and then they splash out all over his face till there are only a few on his ears. His red hair matches his braces too.

I pick out a plain wire cage and head for the reptile section. Sam tags along. Suzy keeps the pinkies in the freezer, and Sam asks what they are when I pull out the package.

"Pinkies," I say.

"They look . . ." He pokes the frozen package with his finger. ". . . kind of gross."

"They're mouse babies. For Peter and Lori, my garter snakes. You defrost 'em in warm water first."

Sam's eyes get real big. "I never knew a girl who liked snakes before."

On the way to the cash register we pass the puppy treats. I realize I actually forgot about the disaster while I was talking to Sam.

I grab a box of the peanut butter ones,

Agnes's favorites, and I feel a pain behind my eyeballs.

"Didn't want the Habitrail, huh?" Suzy says as she scans the cage and the treats.

"Edward G. doesn't deserve it," I say.

When the door swings shut—*meeee-ooowwwww*—it wakes Agnes from her snooze.

"Oh, that's *your* dog," Sam says as I unwind her leash. "What kind is she?"

"Heinz Fifty-seven." I open the box and give Agnes a treat, which she snaps up. The thought of losing her almost brings tears again, but I don't want to cry in front of Sam so I shut my eyes to squeeze them dry.

"What does that mean?" he asks.

"She's a mutt—fifty-seven varieties. Like the catsup," I say.

If I knew Sam better I could tell him all about Mayor Tunnbaum and the letter. He seems like the kind of person who might understand about a dog you grew up with.

For a second the three of us just stand in the yellow light from the Pet Barn sign. "We live that way," I say finally. "On Puma Street."

"Oh," says Sam. "Well, I live over there," and he points the opposite way.

"Well . . . see ya in art," I say.

"Yeah, see ya."

We both walk off, but a minute later I hear my name called.

"Maybe I could come over sometime? To see how you made your rat cages?"

"Yeah, that'd be neat."

"Okay, maybe Thursday," Sam yells.

We wave at each other, and the light from a streetlamp catches his braces, making his smile extra bright.

eleven

On the way home, I start worrying again.

Please please let Doria have convinced Mayor Tunnbaum Agnes isn't vicious. Please please don't let Doria have made things any worse.

Like they could be any worse.

The house is quiet and dark when I walk in the front door.

"Mom?" I call.

"Back here."

I unhook Agnes's leash and give her another treat. She gobbles it, and I give her a third one, which I practically never do. Agnes is pretty fat, and I have to watch her diet for her.

"Oh, Aggie." I bend down and scratch behind those big ears while she chews.

I put Aggie's leash away in my closet, and I don't even stop to check on Robin or spritz Margaret.

My mom is sitting at the kitchen table with all the lights off except a reading lamp. There's a big black book in front of her, and when I look over her shoulder I see it's volume U of the encyclopedia. She's reading the part about the United States Constitution.

"He can't do it," she says to herself. "At least I don't think he can do it. Due process. Or maybe the Fourth Amendment . . ."

"What happened?"

She looks up, and her eyes are all red. For a second, I feel like I should be comforting *her*.

"Nothing good," she says, and looks back down like she doesn't want to talk about it.

"Mom . . ."

"He called me an unfit mother," she says in a little voice. "And he said if our family caused his family any more trouble, he'd re-

86

port me to the proper authorities. Whoever they are."

Maybe I was wrong. Maybe things can get worse.

I put the pinkies in the freezer, and she goes on. She tells me Mrs. Tunnbaum let her in and seemed sort of friendly, said she was sorry about everything. But then Mr. Tunnbaum came in and he didn't even say hello, just started ranting and raving about rabid dogs and unsupervised children roaming the neighborhood in the middle of the night.

I guess he meant Agnes and me.

"Pookie's mother even tried to point out that Agnes was on a leash, but that made the ol' fascist even madder. Finally she left the room," said Doria. "I wouldn't put up with that from *my* husband."

"Didn't you tell him Agnes never bit anybody before? Didn't you tell him I've had her practically my whole life!"

Doria leans her head on her hands and sighs. "I tried to tell him all those things, but there was no getting him to *hear* any of it. In fact, I had a feeling . . . It's like there's something wrong in that house. The vibes are so negative."

"So why did he call you an unfit mother?" I ask.

"It was after Mrs. Tunnbaum walked out. He said anybody who would let their daughter out half undressed . . ."

"But my pajamas cover up practically every inch of my whole body!"

"Then he said something about selling inhalants, like Cinnamon Seminars was some kind of illegal drug." She stops and her face starts to collapse. Here come the tears. "He's a hateful old fascist, Rory. What else can I say?"

"Well, you didn't say anything that did any good."

I feel bad as soon as the words are out, but *honestly*.

I go in the bathroom and get a tissue.

"Thank you." Doria snuffles when I hand it to her. "Sometimes I wonder . . ."

". . . who's the mother in this outfit," we both say, but it doesn't make either one of us smile.

"Anyway," she says, "I'm not done yet. The Constitution says right here in the Fourth Amendment that the government can't seize property without a good reason—"

"Doria," I interrupt her. "They're coming to get Agnes on Thursday—that's day after tomorrow. We studied the Supreme Court in civics, and they don't work that fast."

"We don't need the Supreme Court. Cyril knows a waitress who knows a lawyer who—"

"Mom!" I say, exasperated.

I've decided to do something I never did before. I've decided to call my dad.

twelve

The phone number is in my address book, which I keep in the top drawer of the table by my bed. I have to put my alarm clock on the floor and shift Abby and Costello to get at it. My mice look happy enough for once.

"Dr. Mudd's office," says a mechanical-sounding voice.

"Hello, I need—"

"If this is a medical emergency," the voice continues, and I realize it really *is* a machine, "please hang up and call nine-one-one. If you are a new patient, please hang up and call back during business hours. If you are an existing patient with an urgent medical problem, please press one now. If you are an existing patient and wish to leave a message, please press two now. Thank you very much for calling Dr. Mudd. And please have a nice day."

There's a click, then a faint hiss. I feel like I'm talking to Peter on the phone.

I hang up, think a minute, then call back.

"Dr. Mudd's office . . . ," says the voice, and the whole thing starts over. I press 2.

"Thank you for pressing two," says the voice. "Please leave a message for Dr. Mudd at the sound of the tone. You will have thirty seconds to record your message. And please have a nice day."

"Uh, this is Aurora Mudd, uh . . . Dad . . . and I don't have a medical problem, but I do have a problem, and . . . uh, it's about Agnes and Mayor Tunnbaum. . . . Uh, he wants to arrest her because she bit Pookie. . . . Pookie's his daughter, and she's my best friend, and Agnes broke the skin but only a little and it isn't like she's *rabid* or anything . . . and—"

Click. There's the dial tone again. I guess I talked too long.

I call back and talk faster.

"So-he-wants-to-arrest-her-and-she's-never-bitten-anybody-before-and-she-isn't-a-bit-vicious-she's-too-old-and-I've-had-her-all-my-life-practically-and-if-you-could-talk-to-him-it-might-help-anyway-please-call-me-right-away."

I hang up, put the address book away, straighten the cage, and put the alarm clock on top of it.

So much has happened since school got out today it feels like the middle of the night, but it's really only 10:02. Usually I'd be coming in from my walk with Agnes now.

I just hate having my schedule go all ker-flooey. I haven't even done my math homework yet.

Luckily, graphs are pretty easy, so I get my book. For a few minutes I concentrate on making tiny pencil dots that match up with the x axis and the y axis, and only when I hear Agnes chasing rabbits in her sleep do I remember how terrible everything is.

Maybe my dad will call me back soon—tonight even. And maybe he can do something.

thirteen

I am staring at the ceiling and listening to the *squeak-squeak* of Larry and Vivien, two of my gerbils, taking turns on their whirly-wheel. The alarm clock says 3:27 A.M.

Al Jolson is curled up in a ball on top of my feet, keeping them warm. Rita has been out hunting, but now I hear a bump as she lands on the floor by my bed. She has come up the ramp and in my window. I hope she didn't bring anything with her. Sometimes I find half-eaten "gifts" at the foot of the bed in the morning.

There are no more tears in me, but every time I hear Agnes snort or roll over I get that pain behind my eyeballs. My dad never called back. Probably he will today . . . but what if he doesn't?

I thought of calling Gramma and Pop, but so far grown-ups have not exactly been a huge help.

The letter from Mr. Catpoop, or whatever his name is, is next to me on the bed, and I switch on the nightlight to read it for the zillionth time.

"Aurora Mudd . . . owner of a female mongrel dog, color brown . . ."

All of a sudden, like it has been there all along just waiting for me to pay attention to it, I get an idea.

"Color brown."

I'm awake a little longer after that, trying to make my idea into a plan that will work. Plan A, I name it just before I fall asleep.

The next thing I know, Agnes is poking me with her nose, and it's time to get up.

I take some more birthday money out of my gym sock and stuff a wad, and a few quarters, in the pockets of my blue jeans right before I leave for school.

At snack, I see Pookie on the other side of

the school courtyard, and I head right for her.

"Golly molly, Rory! You look awful!" she says through a mouthful of doughnut. "All puffy and blotchy and circles under your eyes. Like you've been crying. What happened?"

"You don't know?"

"Know what?"

"Your dad! Agnes! Weren't you home when Doria came over?" I can feel tears in my eyes again.

"What are you talking about? Here, I've got a tissue in my pocket. I carry 'em to wipe Barney's nose."

While I blot my eyes I tell her everything.

"I was at my ballet lesson last night," she says. "But maybe that's why—"

"Can't you talk to your dad?" I interrupt her. "Show him your leg is all better?"

"I could talk to him," Pookie says slowly, "if I knew where he was."

Now it's my turn to be shocked. "What are you talking about? Where is he?"

"I don't know," Pookie says. She looks

more confused than sad. "But I guess he must've left after your mom came over."

"He's *left* you?"

"I guess so, yeah." Pookie's voice sounds very small.

My mom always buys the same kind of salt—the kind in the round blue box with the little girl on it—and on the side it says, "When it rains it pours." That's how it seems right now. It's *pouring* catastrophes.

"Did he leave a note or anything?" I ask.

"Mom won't talk about it, and I'm kind of afraid to ask," Pookie says. "But he wasn't home when I got back from ballet, and he wasn't home this morning either."

"Didn't your mom say anything?"

"Not really. She looks terrible. Like you. All puffy. Crying 'er eyes out."

"Oh, man, Pookie, I am *so* sorry. What a terrible day."

"Oh, I'm okay." She brushes a pow-dered-sugar crumb off her jacket and looks up at me for the first time. "It's quieter around the house now at least."

There's the bell and I haven't even had a

chance to ask Pookie to help me with my plan.

But now I think maybe I shouldn't. I mean, she's going through a crisis that might change her entire life. What if her dad disappears forever and they don't have any money and they have to sell their nice house and move into a trailer or something? But on the other hand, maybe I should ask her to help. First, I have to save my dog, and second, it might be good if Pookie had something to think about besides moving to a trailer.

Pookie and I start heading back into the building together.

"What are you going to do about Agnes?" she asks like she's been reading my mind. "I mean, what are *we* going to do?"

"Well, I do have this idea," I say, "but do you really feel like helping me? With your dad and everything?"

"Rory. Best friends. Right?"

"Best friends," I say.

I don't have time to tell her about Plan A right now, but we agree to meet at the Save-A-Bunch on the corner at three-fifteen.

fourteen

Art class is right before lunch. We're making animal sculptures, and mine is an Agnes out of crumpled newspaper. Papier-mâché strips will go over that, then paint and lacquer.

It's been coming along pretty good, but when I sit down and look at my newspaper Agnes, I think about the real Agnes.

"What's the matter?" Sam asks. He's sitting across from me, next to Tiffany Silversmith, who has been wearing makeup since the fourth grade. "You look sick."

"Nothin'," I say. I don't feel like talking about all this with Tiffany right there.

"I had the flu last week and I thought I

was gonna die. Barfed all night and all day. Maybe you're getting it."

"Thank you for sharing," says Tiffany, like she never threw up in her life.

Sam's sculpture looks like a sausage, but he's braiding together three long strings for a tail so I think it's probably a rat.

"I wish it was the flu," I say.

"Worse than the flu? It must be really terrible." He finishes his braid, sticks it on one end of the sausage, looks at it, then sticks it on the other end. "You can tell me, Rory. Unless it's a secret, I mean."

"It's just . . . complicated," I say. I unroll a long strand of masking tape and wrap it around and around the wads of newspaper so they'll stay together. Then I get toilet paper tubes I brought from home and try them on the bottom of my "dog" for legs.

"That's Agnes, isn't it?" says Sam. "It looks just like her. The legs anyway."

"Who's Agnes?" Tiffany asks.

"Her dog," Sam says.

"What kind of dog has legs like *that*?"

"Heinz Fifty-seven," says Sam.

He smiles at me, and I laugh. Tiffany

gives us both these *looks* like we're on a different planet.

The rest of the day passes slowly. When I finally get to the Save-A-Bunch, Pookie's already there, talking on the pay phone on the sidewalk out front.

She's just hanging up when I walk over to her.

"Mom's crying again," she says. "I feel so bad for her. I told her I'd be home soon to help with Barney. He doesn't understand what's going on. Every time she turns around he's run off, and when she tracks him down he says he's looking for Daddy."

I think about Barney, and I get mad. "Why do you think grown-ups are so . . . so *creepy*?" I ask. "They breathe stinky stuff out of marbles, they walk out on their families, then they try to arrest your dog. Kids don't act like that."

Inside we find the aisle labeled HAIR PRODUCTS and scan the shelves looking for the box that will rescue Agnes. There are sure a lot of different kinds, and they have the dumbest names, "Midnight Magic," "Ravishing Raven," "Jazzy Jet."

"What about this one?" Pookie asks, picking up a box. "Black Beauty."

"Yeah, that sounds good," I say. "And it's one of my favorite books."

"Cheaper than the other ones too," says Pookie. "Only twelve ninety-five." She giggles. "I sound like I'm on a commercial."

"If it works, we'll make one," I say. I stand up real straight and pretend my fist is a microphone. " 'Cops after your dog? Disguise her with Black Beauty. They'll never suspect a thing!' "

Pookie laughs so hard a lady putting shampoo in a cart stares at her, and then I laugh too. For about half a minute we both forget all the awful stuff that's happened, and it feels really good.

fifteen

Agnes does not like being dyed.

She is in the sink where I wash her, waiting thirty minutes for the dye to soak in. We have been listening to the tick-tick-tick of the kitchen timer echoing around the garage for twenty-one minutes now. It makes me think of the hourglass the witch gives Dorothy in *The Wizard of Oz*.

About every minute, Agnes shakes herself from head to tail. Between shakes she shivers and whimpers and tries to climb out of the sink.

She looks miserable. Her batwing ears are all droopy, which means she's unhappy, and who can blame her? This is no bath; it smells all wrong—like ammonia instead of grapefruit—and it's taking way longer to get to the toweling-off part than any bath ever does.

I was hoping Pookie could help me, but she called a little while ago. She's stuck home trying to entertain Barney until bedtime. Her mom is sitting on the couch in the family room staring at some really old TV show about a happy family. She's stopped crying, Pookie said, but she doesn't look good.

Pookie said the worst part so far is that they had nothing but microwave popcorn for dinner. Barney thought that was great, but Pookie's starving. They even ran out of Doritos.

I said maybe after Agnes is dry I'll bring Pookie something to eat. Pookie's mom usually does everything. Pookie barely knows how to work the microwave, let alone make a grilled cheese sandwich.

At last the timer dings. It's been thirty minutes.

"Okay, ol' girl. I'm gonna rinse you now."

This is the part I've been worried about.

The directions say that sometimes the dye doesn't take—something to do with "hair chemistry." I didn't know there was such a thing as hair chemistry, but that's what it says. So maybe, when I rinse her off, all the black will come off too.

"In that case we'll go to Plan B," I say to Agnes. "I just hope I can think up Plan B."

When I got home from school today, I thought there'd be a message from my dad. But there wasn't. And then I figured for sure he'd call after work. But he didn't.

Plan A is all I've got.

I aim the water at Agnes's tail first, then slowly bring it up her back to her neck and head. I look down at the bottom of the sink to see if the dye is coming off. The water running down the drain looks gray, but Agnes's fur is still black.

"Here comes the part you like!" I say when she's all rinsed and I'm lifting her out of the sink.

I'm kneeling on the kitchen floor rubbing her down with a white towel when I hear the van in the garage. A minute later Doria comes in the back door. It's the first time

I've seen her since last night. She was asleep when I left for school, and when I got home there was a note on the refrigerator that said she had a Women's Center meeting, and then she was going out to dinner with Cyril.

"What in the world . . . ?" she says when she sees us in the kitchen. "What happened to Agnes?"

"Uh, she's gone," I say. "This is . . . uh . . . This is Garbo."

"Garbo?" Doria says. She kneels beside me. "Nice to meet you, Gar." She sticks out her hand to shake, and "Garbo" puts out her paw too. "Well trained," says Doria. "Just like Agnes. And she has Agnes's eyes too."

"Well, her name is Garbo, okay?"

"And where did you get Garbo?"

"Uh . . . she followed Pookie home, and you know Pookie's parents, they won't let her have even a guppy, and so, uh, she gave her to me."

"And if this is Garbo, where did you say Agnes is?"

"Gone."

"Vanished into thin air?"

"Thin air," I repeat. Maybe I'll have to work on this part of the story before the cops get here tomorrow. "Actually," I say, "I *let* her go. Chased her out of the yard and told her not to come back. That way the cops can't arrest her."

"Was this before or after Garbo arrived?" Doria asks.

"After. No . . . before . . . uh . . . I can't remember exactly."

"You know," she says, "I'm not sure Garbo was quite clean when you got her out of the bath. The towel looks spotted, and so does your T-shirt."

I take the towel by the corners and hold it up to get a good look. It's spotted all over with black, just like my T-shirt. I look like a faded Dalmatian.

Because I've been talking to Doria I haven't been paying that good attention to Agnes—*Garbo*—either. Now I look down at her fur and see it's not solid black like it was when she was wet. She looks sort of like camouflage cloth, but instead of blotchy green she's blotchy black and gray.

"She was a stray so she musta been pretty

106

dirty," I start to say, but suddenly the whole Garbo story sounds way stupid.

I guess Doria can see what I'm thinking, because she sits down next to me and Agnes and puts her arm around my shoulders. "Well, who knows, darling? It might work," she says. "But there is one thing. Don't put her collar back on. The tags identify her, remember?"

"I never woulda thought of that," I say.

Doria gets up and stretches. "Are you hungry?" she asks. "I am."

"I thought you just went out to dinner."

"We never got around to eating," she says, staring into the refrigerator.

"Does that mean you were too busy smooching or something?" The idea of smooching with Mr. Cinnamon is really sick.

Doria laughs, but it's not a happy sound. "Fighting, more like," she says.

"Oh, good! I mean . . ."

"What are the names of those gerbils again? The ones with the unhappy relationship?" She gets out a couple of carrots and a jug of milk.

"They're not gerbils—they're mice. Abby and Costello."

"Well, I think Abby has the right idea. I should've taken a bite out of his ear."

sixteen

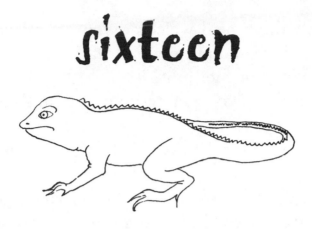

The clock over the stove says nine o'clock. Pookie will be up late, so I look in the cupboard until I find a box of macaroni and cheese in back. Then I get some hot dogs—real ones, not the tofu kind—out of the refrigerator. No sense bringing an apple or anything healthy. Pookie wouldn't touch it.

If I leave now, I might miss my dad's call. But Pookie needs to eat.

"I'm going to Pookie's," I tell Doria, who is sitting at the kitchen table thumbing through *Vegetarian Today* and eating her carrots.

"But what about Mayor Tunnbaum? I

don't think he'd welcome you after I was over there and put my foot in it."

"Put your foot in it?"

"Well, as you pointed out, I didn't help matters any."

"Oh, Doria," I say. "I didn't mean it. I was just upset. At least you tried."

"I did try," she says. "But do you really think it's a good idea to go over there into enemy territory—I mean to Pookie's house?"

"Oh gosh, you don't know!" I say, and I explain how Pookie's dad just disappeared.

"I knew the vibes were all wrong. Maybe they need *feng shui*. You might suggest it."

"*Feng* what?"

She tells me that's a Chinese thing where someone comes and figures out if a house is in harmony with the earth. *Honestly.* I can just see trying to tell Pookie's parents about *that*.

"Outta here," I say.

As I walk down the hall, I hear Doria call, "May the moon goddess illuminate your path!"

"Stay, Ag—I mean Garbo," I say at the front door. Agnes cocks her head and looks puzzled. "Strange night for you, isn't it, ol' girl?" I kneel down to scratch her head.

As I walk around the corner to Pookie's house, I am thinking *Garbo Garbo Garbo*.

At the Tunnbaums' house, I knock softly on the back door, the one into the kitchen, hoping I'll get Pookie's attention instead of her mom's. I remember what Pookie said about how her mom and dad think I'm a bad influence.

But when the light goes on, it's Mrs. Tunnbaum's face I see through the window in the door. Like Pookie said, she looks awful.

"What are you doing here, Aurora? At this hour?" Even her voice sounds funny. Deep and sort of dead, like she isn't interested in what she's saying.

"Pookie's hungry," I say. I hold up the paper bag. "I brought her some food."

"Hungry?"

"Can I come in?" I ask. She seems stuck somehow. "I won't stay long. I just thought

I'd fix her some macaroni and cheese. See?" I pull out the box, thinking maybe seeing it will help her understand what I'm saying.

"Hungry . . . ," she repeats, stepping aside so I can get past her. Then, like she finally remembers what the word *hungry* means, she makes this little noise, a sob I guess. "My husband's gone and my children are going hungry. . . ."

"Barney's okay," I say quickly, wanting to reassure her. "He really *liked* having popcorn for dinner. And I can feed this to Pookie. They'll be okay. Uh, are you hungry? I brought hot dogs too."

Mrs. Tunnbaum looks at me so hard with her bloodshot eyes that I start to feel embarrassed. Then she says, real gently, "Thank you, Rory. You don't need to feed me, honey. But thank you."

It's almost eerie the quiet way she walks off. In a second I hear a door click shut someplace down the hall, and then Pookie's sneakers squeaking on the kitchen floor.

"Golly molly, what a night! I just got Barney into bed, and I'm not guaranteeing he'll stay there even now. Did Mom let you in? Where is she?''

"In her bedroom, I think. I heard the door close. Do you . . . ?''

I'm still holding the box, and Pookie spots it before I can finish my question. "Macaroni and cheese!'' she says. "My absolute favorite! Golly, Rory, thank you! Do you know how to make it?''

I roll my eyes. "Pookie,'' I say, "the directions are on the back. You just have to know how to read.''

"Oh, I'm no good at that kind of thing. I'd burn it or something. I'll watch.''

She takes a seat at the kitchen table while I get a couple of pans out of the cupboard next to the stove and find a measuring cup.

I melt butter while the water heats up for the macaroni. I tell Pookie Agnes is now black and what a pain it was to dye her. Pookie says she just knows Plan A will work. Then she starts telling me about a boy with freckles who she likes. I'm wondering if it's Sam when I feel these little arms clench my knees. I'm so surprised I almost pour the orange powdery stuff in his hair.

"Hi, Wohwy!"

"Bernard Tunnbaum!" says Pookie at practically the same instant. "You are supposed to be in bed, young man!"

I am always amazed at what a good imitation Pookie can do of her father.

"Hi, Barney," I say, when the powder's stirred into the butter and I can look down at him. He's still got hold of my knees and he's smiling at me with that sweet face of his, cute as one of my gerbils, almost.

Pookie doesn't seem to have the energy to actually haul him back to bed. She'd rather just scold him. "What's Mommy going to say if she finds you up?"

"Mommy c'y c'y c'y aw day," Barney tells me solemnly. It takes a second before I realize he's saying his mom cried all day.

"I know, Barney," I say because I don't know what else to say. "It'll be okay."

"Daddy aw gone," he says.

I'm about ready to add my tears to the macaroni. But, with Barney still holding tight, I manage to hobble across the kitchen, drain the macaroni into the sink, hobble back, and dump it in with the sauce.

"Do you want a plate?" I ask Pookie.

"I'm too hungry to wait that long," she says, getting to her feet and taking the pan from me.

"Wait for a fork at least," I say, handing her one. "Barney, do you want me to take you back to bed?"

"Yeah! Wohwy bed! Wohwy bed!" he shouts.

"You don't need to," Pookie says. Her teeth are kind of glued together by the cheese, and her voice sounds sticky. "I'll take him when I'm done."

"It's okay. We're friends, huh, Barn? Come on."

Barney's room is next to Pookie's on the second floor. Of course, it's full of cats—a poster of a lion and her cubs next to the window, a photo of a springing tiger framed on the bureau, and stuffed cougars, kittens, leopards, and panthers on the bed, which is covered with a jungle bedspread.

"Get in. Go on," I say. "No tricks!"

"Wead me book," he says.

"Please."

"Wead me book *p'eez*, Wohwy."

115

Grown-ups say little kids are rude, but I say little kids are parrots.

There's a pile of books on the floor by Barney's bed—most of them about cats—and I grab the skinniest one. It has something to do with a baby dinosaur that runs away and meets a saber-toothed tiger. It seems kind of scary for a bedtime story. Barney falls asleep before I find out what happens.

I turn on the nightlight and kiss him good night on his chubby little cheek. I've just clicked the light switch when I hear the sheets rustle.

"I lubboo, Wohwy," he says.

"I love you too."

seventeen

If you could flunk out of school in one day, I would have done it today. I erased half my answers on the math test and didn't have time to go back and fill in new ones. I spelled *ocelot* with an *s* in the first round of the spelling bee. In civics, Ms. Schuyler asked me how come I hadn't turned a page yet when I'd been staring at the book for half an hour.

Now finally the last bell is ringing and I can meet Pookie and we can go home.

I just hope Agnes is still black when we get there.

We're almost to my corner when Pookie tells me she called her dad's office at lunch to see if he was there.

"That was a smart idea," I say. "Was he?"

"No, but his secretary said he'd be back at one-thirty and did I want to leave a message," she says.

"What did you say?"

"I just mumbled, 'No thank you,' and hung up."

"Are you gonna tell your mom you called him?" I ask.

I'm thinking about how I called my dad and didn't want to tell my mom. He still hasn't called back. And now it's too late.

"I don't think so," Pookie says.

We climb the steps to the front door, and I can hear Agnes—I mean *Garbo*—barking on the other side.

"Down, Agnes! Down! Down!" Pookie yells as the door opens. "Wow, she really looks different! You did a great job, Rory."

Still looking like camouflage cloth, Agnes is jumping all over both of us. She's so heavy she knocks me backward. "Oh, man, Pookie. You *can't* call her Agnes. Remember? She's Garbo now—to fool the Animal Control cops."

"Down, Garbo!" Pookie says obediently.

"Hello-o-o-o!" Doria's voice comes from down the hall. In a second, she appears in the doorway to the living room. She smiles hello, but then her face gets all funny. "What's all over your Levi's?" she asks. Then she looks over at Pookie. "Black smudges on you too. They look like pawprints."

Sure enough, Pookie and I are spotted where Garbo jumped on us.

"The dye must be rubbing off!" Pookie says.

"What time are they supposed to be here?" Doria asks.

"Between four and five, the letter said. So she doesn't have to be black much longer."

"Plenty of time yet," Doria says.

"Time for what?" I ask.

"Never mind, darling. Everything's going to be fine. Do you know what you're going to tell them?"

"Sort of."

"You answer the door then. But I'll be here if you need me."

Pookie's hungry so we head for the kitchen, with Garbo click-clicking along behind. She settles in under the kitchen table while I get a kiwi fruit out of the refrigerator and cut up half for Margaret Hamilton, half for Pookie and me.

Pookie says, "Yuck. Don't you have any Pop-Tarts or anything?"

I climb up on a stool to look in the cupboards—sometimes Doria stashes a box of Oreos up high so she won't eat them all at once—and just as I'm stretched to the max and feeling around on the top shelf, the doorbell rings.

Agnes races for the front door, barking up a storm. "Just a minute!" I yell. I climb down as fast as I can and I'm in the hallway when I hear Doria open the door.

"Down, Garbo," she says, then, "What a surprise! Come in," which doesn't sound like she's talking to a dogcatcher.

". . . sometime this week, so I just thought I'd stop by on my way home from school and see if by chance . . . ," says a man's voice from the living room. It sounds a little familiar, and then I realize who it is, and I smile even though this might turn out to be the worst afternoon of my life.

In the kitchen, Pookie's up on the stool feeling around on the high shelf for Oreos. "Nothing but granola bars," she says, disgusted. "Who was it?"

"Mr. Goode," I say.

"Can I peek?" Pookie asks.

"Go in the dining room and open the door a crack."

Pookie does, and when I look in I see her kneeling by the door with her head halfway in the living room. If they see her it'll be *so* embarrassing. "Pookie!" I whisper, but she doesn't hear.

I'm wondering if I should tap her on the shoulder when the doorbell rings again. This time it *has* to be the cops.

"*Stay!*" I say to Ag . . . I mean Garbo. "And be *quiet!*"

My heart's pounding as I walk down the hall. I open the door, and . . . it's not a dogcatcher but *Sam* standing on the front step.

"At the Pet Barn we talked about the rat cages and you said Thursday was okay and . . ." He puts his hands in his pockets and looks at his feet.

121

I scan the street, left and right. No dog-catcher wagon. "Come in quick," I say. I grab his wrist and pull so he practically falls into the house with this real surprised look on his face.

Doria appears behind me in the hall. "Is everything okay?" she says.

"So far."

"And who is this?"

"Sam," I say. "From art class."

"Oh yes, the good dribbler. Nice to meet you."

"This is my mom—Doria."

"Nice to meet you," Doria says again.

"Oh, yeah . . . hi," says Sam, like his mouth has come unstuck.

"Mr. Goode is interested in sampling a couple more Cinnamon Seminar products," Doria says. "I'll be in the living room."

"I'm sorry," I say to Sam. "Come on and I'll explain. It's a really strange day. A terrible day. Do you like kiwi fruit?" Any other time I would be really *glad* to see Sam and show him Gerbil City and help him with a cage and everything, but today of all days . . .

When the doorbell rings again, Sam is sitting at the kitchen table eating a granola bar, Garbo is waiting under Sam's chair in case there are crumbs, and Pookie is still glued to the conversation in the living room.

"Stay, Garbo," I say.

"Is that them?" Sam asks. By now I've had a chance to explain that the cops are coming for my dog.

"Gotta be," I say. I can feel my chest getting tight again.

"You want me to back you up?" Sam asks.

"Okay."

With Sam behind me in the hallway, I take a deep breath . . . open the door, and . . . there's Gramma.

"She doesn't look like a dogcatcher," Sam whispers.

"What are you doing here?" I ask, then I remember Sam and introduce them.

"To answer your question," Gramma says, "your mother called this morning and said something about police and Agnes and asked if I was free. What was she talking about? And what *is* that smell?"

"The one they make tea out of—camomile, I think," I answer. I'm explaining how Mr. Goode came by for his chocolate spray when Doria comes in.

Probably the worst day of my life, and it's like *party time* in the hallway.

"Come on in the living room, Mother," Doria says. Then she pulls me aside. "Why is Pookie hiding behind the dining room door?" she whispers. I don't know how to answer that one, and she goes on in a regular voice, "We'll stay out of your way, Rory. I just called your gramma because I thought we might need—" She pauses like she's trying to think of the right word. "—reinforcements," she says at last.

eighteen

The next time the doorbell rings, it's Mr. Cinnamon.

Why not? I'm thinking. Join the fun on the worst afternoon of my life.

"I'm just here to pick up the remaining Cinnamon Seminars paraphernalia," he says. "I guess your mother told you that once these orders are filled, her term of employment with my company will be at an end?"

"Actually, we've been pretty busy," I say. Doria comes and says hello real serious; then they go into the living room.

In my room, meanwhile, the camomile smell has made Gerbil City crazy. Margaret's climbing around on her manzanita branch; Gregory, the cockatiel, is flapping his wings and squawking, while Cassidy, the rabbit, is doing her whirling dervish trick: *thumpa-thumpa-thumpa-thumpa* clockwise, *thumpa-thumpa-thumpa-thumpa* counterclockwise.

"She makes me dizzy just watching!" says Sam.

Abby and Costello are going at it, too—*EEEEEE-eeeeep EEEEEE-eeeeep*—but this time Costello seems to be winning. Peck is flapping his wings and opening his beak like he wants to say something, but it isn't "Attagirl." Even Al Jolson, who usually couldn't care less, is mewing and poking at the cages under my nightstand, the ones with mouse granddaughters and grandsons. I have to shoo him away with my foot.

Only Agnes, lying at the foot of my bed snoozing, is quiet. Well, Agnes and the fish.

"It's not usually this noisy," I apologize to Sam. "But the smells get them nuts. When Doria had her Cinnamon Seminar, you should've seen what Agnes did and all the trouble I got in."

Sam is looking in each of the cages like he's never seen an animal before. When he gets to Margaret he jumps back a little.

"Iguana," I say. "Margaret Hamilton." She blinks her eyes lazily, the closest thing to hello I ever get from her. "She must like you."

"You take care of all of them?" he asks. "By yourself?"

"Well, yeah." Now I'm kind of embarrassed. Maybe he does think I'm weird.

"How come?"

"I dunno. I never really thought about it," I say. "I guess . . . I guess I wanted to make a family for myself. I mean, Doria's an okay mom, but we're not a family the way some kids have families."

"So instead of brothers and sisters and a dad, you have gerbils," says Sam, "not to mention guinea pigs and mice and hamsters and birds . . ."

". . . and a pregnant rat, a rabbit, two toads, an iguana, two cats, a dog, *und*"—I motion to the other terrarium—"garter snakes!"

"Wow!" says Sam, watching Peter and Lori slither over each other. "I'd take them over *my* brother and sister any day!"

Sam is offering Margaret kiwi fruit when the doorbell rings again. Practically everybody I know is already at my house. This time it must be for real.

Agnes pokes her head up. "Stay, Garbo," I say, and she puts it back down again.

Walking down the hall, listening to my heart thump, I wonder for the first time what the cops will look like. I picture big fat men, little pig eyes and crooked yellow teeth, black uniforms and huge gold badges with snarling cougar heads on them. They'll have nets, and they'll have their guns out and pointed right at me.

I open the front door, hoping they don't shoot me by mistake or anything . . .

. . . and behind the door are two pretty women, one blond and one dark-haired, wearing pale blue uniforms. They have straight teeth. Little badges. No net. On their belts, each carries something that might be a very small gun, but I don't get a good look.

"Are you Aurora Mudd?" asks the one on the left, the dark-haired one. She has a gentle voice, and she looks sympathetic. Like she doesn't think arresting a kid's dog is really all that fun.

"Yes," I say, or rather croak. I sound like Hedda, the toad in the bathtub.

"I guess you know why we're here," she says. "I'm afraid we've been ordered to retrieve your dog, uh . . ." She takes a piece of paper out and looks at it. "Your dog, Agnes," she says.

"She's not here," I say. My voice sounds a little stronger now. The two women look at each other. "She ran away last night. I mean afternoon. She's gone is what I mean."

"Honey," says the other woman, the blond one. If anything, her voice is even gentler. "I know this is really hard for you. We don't like it either. But when a dog turns vicious, we have to keep the public safety in mind first, and in this . . ." She pauses, then says, "What is that unusual smell? It's sort of like . . ."

She is still talking, but I'm no longer paying attention because I smell it, too, a smell that is *really* disgusting and also *really* familiar. At first, I don't believe it, but then I hear a yowl from the bedroom—like a seal barking.

And my heart starts pounding again.

Cougar Musk.

What happens next takes about a zillionth of a second. There's another yowl, then Sam's voice, "No, Garbo! Down!", then his sneakers thudding and Agnes's toenails clicking as he chases her.

"Aaaarrrh aaaarrrh aaaarrrh!" Agnes howls from the living room, where I hear chair legs scraping and Cyril Cinnamon's panicky voice: "Get her away from me! Get that vicious beast away from me!"

"Rory!" calls Doria.

"Just a minute," I say to the two officers, who look about as surprised as I am. "I'll be right back."

As I turn, there's this brilliant flash of light that makes my shadow on the wall in front of me. "Hey, what the—" says one of the cops, but I don't look back.

The living room is chaos, with Agnes at the center of it all, howling.

Pookie's on the floor, Mr. Cinnamon's standing on a chair, and everybody else—Sam, Doria, Gramma, and Mr. Goode—is yelling at Agnes to get her to shut up.

"Agnes, Agnes, come on, puppy," my gramma is saying, while Doria says "Garbo" and "Agnes" about half and half. My poor dog is so confused she probably doesn't know what her name is anymore. I sure hope the cops at the door don't have very good hearing.

"Arrrh-aaaarrrh-arrrh!" Agnes cries.

Before I can do anything, there's another flash of light, and this time I turn around to see what in heck it is.

Oh man!

The Animal Control cops are right behind me—standing in the living room! By now they've heard everybody call my dog Agnes.

So much for Plan A.

Behind them I see the reason for the flashes—it's a camera. My mom's friend Chris, the one who works at the newspaper, is shooting pictures. Why he's there is more than I can figure out right now. I just

131

hope my vicious dog doesn't make page one.

What with the flashes and the seal bark and Mr. Cinnamon screeching, things are completely out of control when one of the cops, the blond one, speaks up.

"I don't think there's anything to be afraid of," she says calmly, looking right at Mr. Cinnamon. Her voice has an instant effect—on both him and Agnes.

They stop howling.

"Ms. Mudd?" says the other cop. "Is that Agnes?"

"*No!*" I say, knowing it's hopeless. "It's Garbo, a whole different dog."

"You see," says Doria, "she's black, and Agnes . . ."

But I can see from their faces they aren't believing it, and the blond cop unclips a muzzle from her belt.

Agnes is trapped. There's only one thing to do.

"Run, Agnes, run!" I yell, and I race at her, stampeding her out of the living room and down the hall. I keep after her, yelling and stamping, until she makes a tremendous leap onto my bed, jumps past Margaret on the windowsill, and charges down the cat plank to freedom.

"Go, Agnes! Go! Get away! Don't come back!" I yell out the window, and I don't even realize I'm sobbing until my voice chokes up and I can't yell anymore.

Agnes is running up the Puma Street sidewalk, but she keeps looking back, and that slows her down. Any second, I figure, I am going to see one of those kind, pretty cops chase her down, maybe fling a net over her.

But now there's another weird noise—an electronic squeal that pauses and repeats over and over, like a code. It's coming from inside the house, the living room I think. I look out the window one more time—Agnes is out of sight by now—and then, wiping the tears off my face with my sleeve, I go to see what in heck is happening now.

Mr. Cinnamon and Chris are gone. Gramma is collapsed in a chair, and Pookie is leaning against the wall looking dazed. I think Agnes must've knocked her over. In the hall, I can hear Doria apologizing to Mr. Goode. The squealy noise has stopped, and the dark-haired cop is on the phone.

"They were about to chase after Agnes when they got beeped," says Sam. "The little beepers on their belts?"

"Honey?" the blond cop puts her hand on my shoulder. "You and your dog are off the hook, but only for now. We don't have time to look for her. They've got a citywide call out for practically everybody in uniform. Big emergency."

I am so relieved I guess I grin, and she looks at me sternly. "That wasn't a very smart thing you did. Agnes might get run over by a car, or get into a fight with another dog and get hurt."

And she *might* get away, I think. Her odds are better than they were with you. But I try to straighten out my smile.

"What's the emergency?" Sam asks. I am so happy about Agnes's good luck, I don't even care.

But a second later, I forget all about Agnes.

"Kid disappeared," says the dark-haired cop. "Very important kid who lives right around the corner—Bernard Tunnbaum, Jr.," she says, "the mayor's little boy."

nineteen

After the cops left, Sam walked Pookie home to be with her mom, and Gramma left to drive around and look for Barney. It hardly seems to matter now, but Doria says the Cougar Musk got out because Mr. Goode wanted to sample Luscious Lemon.

"I used the marbles in the packet marked 'Lemon,' but the smell turned out to be Cougar Musk," she said. "I don't understand it."

"Oh, *no*," I groaned. "The lemon ones were almost the same color as Cougar Musk. I was hurrying when I put things away after your Cinnamon Seminar. I must've mixed them up. It's all my fault."

"Don't be too hard on yourself, darling, Doria said.

Then I remembered the flash.

"What about Chris—taking pictures? How did he get here?"

"Well, it seemed like a good idea at the time," Doria said. "I figured if you couldn't convince the cops that Agnes was really Garbo, maybe a headline that said, 'Cops haul away little girl's dog, claim she's vicious,' with a picture of innocent-looking Agnes might force the mayor to back down."

"Now the picture will show Agnes terrifying a roomful of people instead," I said.

"Looks like I put my foot in it again."

A few minutes later, Doria went off to her room to meditate.

Now I'm sitting on the floor staring at the purple case that says CINNAMON SEMINARS.

I am not thinking about anything really, just kind of worrying about Barney, thinking how cute he looked last night—curled up with all his stuffed kitties in bed—remembering when he was lost at the zoo, and how he went straight for the "big kitties. . . ."

137

The big kitties.

Of course, they might have found Barney by now. Or he might be someplace obvious and safe like under his bed or in the attic. Anyway, he couldn't possibly walk that far by himself. . . . He couldn't possibly be . . .

Except all at once, I know absolutely for certain where he *is*. And I've gotta hurry.

I'm almost through the door when I get this idea that might turn out to be really helpful when I get where I'm going. So I rush back into the living room, grab the Cinnamon Seminars briefcase with all the marbles in it, and sling its strap over my shoulder.

"Leaving, Doria," I yell, and without waiting for an answer I'm gone.

It's dark already. Dark and cold. I don't like to think of Barney out by himself at night. I hope he has a jacket with him at least.

I start out running as fast as I can down Puma Street, dodging tricycles and plastic ponies.

By the time I get to Dingo Boulevard, I'm

hot and sweaty and my lungs ache from too much breathing. I don't want to slow down, but my legs feel heavy and so does the stupid Cinnamon Seminars bag I've got bumping against my side.

I cross Zoo Drive and make a left toward the entrance. The gates are locked, and there's a big red sign on the fence, ZOO CLOSED.

But it's only a plain fence, no barbed wire or anything. I look right and left to see that nobody else is on the sidewalk just at the moment—I don't have time to be explaining to anybody what I'm doing.

Somebody honks their horn just as I throw my leg over the top. It startles me and I nearly fall, but the strap of the Cinnamon Seminars bag catches on some pointy wires and holds me long enough to get my balance again. I climb down a couple of steps, then drop to the asphalt and start running.

In the distance I can hear one of the seals barking—"arrrrh-aaarrrrrh-aaaaaarrrrrrh!" It's very nearly dark now, but the moon gives me enough light that I can see the path in front of me. The big cat enclosures are just past the gift shop on the right.

The seal's bark is getting louder, which is weird because they keep the seals way over on the other side of the zoo.

There's the first of the cat cages, the tiger cage. I look inside and can barely make out the long form of the tiger, stretching. Next is the cougar cage, where they're working on the new "habitat."

"Barney!" I yell.

No answer. There's a yellow ribbon barrier again, and a pile of gravel behind it that I can't see around. I duck under the plastic ribbon and run around the gravel so I can see the fence and beyond it, the cougar's unfinished enclosure.

"*Arrrrh-aaarrrrrh-aaaaaarrrrrrh!*" There's that seal again, sounding like it's right in the cage with the cougar.

I peer inside, trying to focus in the moonlight. Oh man, there *is* something in there with the cougar, but it doesn't look like a little boy, it looks more like . . .

"*Arrrrh-aaarrrrrh-aaaaaaarrrrrrh!*"

Agnes!

She's got four paws planted in the middle of the enclosure, her nose aimed right at the moon, and she's howling to keep the cougar in his corner!

"Agnes!" I yell, and she looks in my direction for a second, but when the cougar see his chance he swipes at her and she starts seal-barking again.

"Wohwy, Wohwy, he'p." The voice is so faint I hardly hear it.

"Barney? Where are you?"

"He'p. *P'eeeeeez.*"

There he is.

In the darkest part of the enclosure, opposite the cougar with Agnes between them. Suddenly I realize why Agnes is so determined to keep that cougar back—she's protecting Barney.

"Don't worry, Barney! I'm coming!"

Midway up the fence I remember why I brought the marbles. Holding on to the fence with one hand, I unzip the bag and look inside for the plastic package labeled LUSCIOUS LEMON. With the mix-up, the Cougar Musk marbles must be inside. Maybe, just maybe, if I smell like another cougar, the real one will give me enough space to get Barney out.

Here's the package, right on top. I drop the rest of the bag, rip the plastic open with my teeth, then smash a whole handful of the stinky, disgusting things right into my hair. They break like reptile eggs, and the oil oozes and drips down my forehead and neck.

"Wohwy," Barney's little voice is whimpering now.

In a second I've dropped down over the fence and I'm facing the biggest kitty I've ever seen, not twenty feet away. When he sees me, he stops pacing, but his tail keeps up its swishing.

"Nice kitty," I say, sidestepping along the fence toward Barney on the other side of the cage. "Ni-i-i-i-i-ice kitty."

The cougar, holding me in his gaze, takes a cautious step forward, then lowers his shoulders and wiggles his rear end, the same way Rita and Al do when they're ready to pounce on a gopher.

But then, like the wind has changed or something, he lifts up his nose and sniffs the air. Is the Cougar Musk working? Now he stretches his front legs and pads in my direction—still sniffing.

Behind me, I hear something—voices maybe, but all my concentration is focused on the cougar. He's only fifteen feet away . . . even in the dim light, I can see the soft pink of his nose edged in black, his white muzzle, the moonlight glinting on his whiskers . . . ten feet, five feet . . .

The cougar is sniffing my sneakers. I shut my eyes so at least I don't have to see myself die. . . .

Now he's standing up so he can sniff my head. His paws, one on each side of my neck, are leaned up against the fence so I'm trapped. I can feel his whiskers tickling my cheek and his soft nose against my ear. . . . I swear, if he *licks* me . . .

But all at once the cougar's gone, and there's this jumbled confusion of noise—a snarl, a growl, shouting, the blast of a gun, Barney's scream . . . then, miraculously, Barney's laughter.

For a moment after, everything is quiet— except my heart pounding.

"It's okay, honey," says a woman's voice, and I open my eyes. The cougar is lying in front of me, panting with his tongue hanging out, wide eyes glazed. There's a dart drooping from his shoulder. A man in a zookeeper's uniform throws a net over him, and he barely stirs. Agnes is standing right next to them both, her bat ears raised to show she's confused.

"Barney?" I say, and at the same instant, I feel his chubby little arms clasp me around the knees.

"Big ki'y as'eep!" He points to the stunned cougar. "Eat Ba'ney all up!" He laughs like the whole thing has been a huge joke.

"What . . . what happened?" For the first time I look up to see who it is standing beside me, and it's the blond Animal Control officer from this afternoon. She's got a rifle slung over her shoulder.

"Agnes saved your life," she says. "And Barney's too."

"Agnes? But your gun . . ."

"I shot the cougar with the tranquilizer dart, but in this light, I couldn't get a clear

144

shot until Agnes jumped on him and he turned away from you . . ."

"Agnes jumped on the cougar?"

The pretty woman smiles. "I guess it would've been funny if it weren't life-or-death," she says. "A little dog like her attacking a big cat like him. When he leaned up against the fence to sniff your head, she sprang right at his throat, only what she hit was more like his tail. That made him twist around so I could fire."

"How did you even know I was here?" I ask.

"Someone saw a girl climbing the zoo fence," she says. "They called the police. Once we were inside, we heard Agnes's howling and decided to check it out first."

I kneel down to pet my dog and give Barney a hug. "C'mere, Agnes. Good girl. Good ol' girl."

"Honey?" says the officer. "Uh, if you don't mind my asking, what is that stuff all over your head? It stinks to high heaven."

twenty

"He is so ridiculous." *Splat.*
"Ridiculous. Ridiculous. Ridiculous." *Splat*—the last bit of foam hits the sink. I rinse and growl at myself in the mirror. Pretty scary. But not nearly as scary as Agnes the Cougar Dog.

It's Mr. Tunnbaum who's ridiculous. He wants Agnes to have a parade. Agnes and me. *Honestly.*

I put the cap back on the tube of toothpaste and put it away. In the bathtub, Hopper and Hedda are out of crickets, so I drop two in.

Mr. Tunnbaum has been home for three whole days now, and Pookie says for the first day and a little more, he and her mother didn't yell at all.

Now it's more like normal, she says.

Barney made his mom put away all the kitty stuff in his bedroom as soon as the police took him home, but now he's asking for a real cat. I have a feeling he'll get one.

I go out to the garage to get some newspaper to line Edward G.'s new cage, and when I come back the phone is ringing.

"Rory! It's for you!" Doria calls.

Not another one! I never knew there were so many newspapers and TV people in the whole entire world.

Doria hands me the phone. She has a funny look on her face.

"Are we live?" I say. Sometimes talk shows put you on the air with no warning. I was nervous the first couple of times, but now I'm getting used to it.

"Are we *what*? Aurora, is that you?" The voice is sort of familiar, and for a second I think it's somebody I've heard on the radio.

"Yes, this is Aurora Mudd, owner of Agnes the Cougar Dog. Look, I'm sorry, but could we make this quick? One of my rats just pupped, and I've got to move Edward G. into his new cage. . . ."

"Aurora, it's me—your dad. I was just calling to say—"

"Dad?" The word feels funny in my mouth.

"Yes, sweetie. I just wanted to say that Kate and I were so proud when we read all about you and saw it on the news and NPR and everything."

Kate. That's his wife. I always forget her name.

"Thank you."

"Tell me, is Agnes . . . is she the dog I gave you before I . . . uh, when you were a baby?"

"That's the one," I say. "She's the only dog I have."

I pause a second to get up my nerve, then I ask him. "So why didn't you call me back? I was desperate. *Why didn't you call me?*"

"Oh, sweetie, I'm sorry. I've just been so busy. I took out two gallbladders and a thyroid yesterday, and then Kate was having a dinner party for one of the partners. . . . I didn't get to it. Anyway, you handled everything just fine on your own, didn't you?"

I am breathing hard, and my heart's pounding. It's like I'm back in the cougar cage. "I'm not *supposed* to handle everything on my own!" I practically yell. *"I am a kid! Sometimes I need a little help!"*

There is a long pause on the other end of the phone, and I expect to hear a dial tone and a hiss. But finally he says, "I'm sorry. I'm sorry about everything, sweetie. I know that's not enough. Doria and I . . . maybe one day you and I'll be able to talk about all that. Sometimes two people just have to be apart. I made a clean break, started over. I guess I thought as long as I supported you with money, it was okay. But I was fooling myself. Wasn't I?"

I can tell by the way he says it he's hoping I'll just say, No problem. I'm fine. A hero even. Kids don't really need dads when you get right down to it. But I don't.

"Yeah, you were fooling yourself."

Another long pause, then: "Look, sweetie, Kate and I . . . we were wondering if you might want to come for a week-end sometime."

"I dunno," I say. I'm calmer now. "It'd be weird, sort of. I . . . I mean, I hardly know you."

"Or even dinner?" he says. "It's only a couple of hours. Maybe your grandmother and I could meet halfway."

"Maybe sometime, Dad. Sometime could be good. But I'll have to get used to the idea first."

He asks some questions about Robin and the pups, then says he has to go. He and Kate are going to a wedding reception.

"Call me," he says. He gives me his home number, and I write it on the back of the only slip of paper in my pocket, the receipt for the rat cage. "Call anytime, and we'll get together. I mean it, Aurora."

I'm feeding Robin a carrot stick a little later when Doria comes into my room. The pups, all six of them, are doing fine. They're pink and wriggly, healthy as can be. Edward G. is safely in his own cage next door.

"How was that? Talking to your father?" she asks.

"He wants me to visit."

I turn around to look at her. She looks good. She's wearing a T-shirt I gave her one Mother's Day with a blue-jean skirt, and she even has on earrings.

"All I have to do is make the national news to get my dad to notice me."

"So are you going?"

"Do you think I should?" I ask.

"That's not the point."

"I know, but it matters to me. Would your feelings be hurt?"

"Yes," she says. "But I still think maybe you should. Your dad isn't a wicked person, Rory. Even if what he did was terrible—and it was. And you *are* like him in some ways. Can't be helped." She leans down and looks in the rat cage with me. "New residents of Gerbil City."

"Not for long. Sam's gonna come over later and I'm gonna show him how to build a cage. When they're big enough, I think I'll give him a couple of the new ones. He's been wanting a rat."

"Giving gerbils away? That's a first. How come?"

151

"I dunno. I guess maybe I don't need quite such a *big* animal family. After all, I've got a human family. You and me."

Doria's face starts the collapse that means tears, and really, I don't think I can stand it. "Mo-o-o-om . . ."

"I'm sorry, darling."

"Let me get you a tissue."

"No, that's okay. See?" She pulls one out of her pocket. "I've got my own this time. Anyway, I came in here to tell you something. You know I'm giving up Cinnamon Seminars?"

"Right."

"Well, I've heard of a really wonderful new business opportunity. Asian house geckoes," she says. "Cute little lizards! You just let a couple of them loose in your house, and you never have to worry about bugs again! They eat them! All natural! I raise them in the garage, and sell them door-to-door. Russell already said he might be interested."

"Russell?"

"Mr. Goode," she says. "You know, from

your school. We're going out to dinner Friday to talk geckoes.''

Back in the days of Alfred, when we watched *Gone With the Wind*, I liked the character Scarlett O'Hara. Scarlett is not a perfect person and she pretty much deserves the things that happen to her, but one thing about her, she never gives up. Anyway, by the end of the movie her kid is dead and her husband has left her.

But Scarlett won't quit. And the last thing she says is, ''Tomorrow is another day.''

Well, right now Doria reminds me of Scarlett. She *is* about the most embarrassing mom you could imagine. I mean, it would just be so *nice* to have a mother who cooks meals and has a regular job and doesn't wear tie-dyed sweats in public.

But Doria's there when I need her. And maybe I'm learning something from her. Maybe we're even learning from each other.

Robin has finished the carrot and now she's curled up in a pile of sawdust so the pups can nurse.

"Fine-looking gerbils," Doria says.

"Mom," I say, real patient. "They're rats. Long tails. They don't look a thing like gerbils."

"Fine-looking *rats*," she says.

There's a flutter of wings from the cockatiel cage above us, then a sort of squawk, and then, like he was just waiting for the right moment, Peck sings out loud and clear: "Attagirl! Attagirl! Attagirl!"